Through the Mirror

Written by G. M. Berrow

ORCHARD

ORCHARD BOOKS

First published in 2013 in the United States by Little, Brown and Company
First published in Great Britain in 2014 by The Watts Publishing Group
This edition published in 2016 by The Watts Publishing Group

11

A CIP catalogue record for this book is available from the British Library.

ISBN 978 1 40833 6601

Printed and bound by CPI Group (UK) Ltd, Croydon, CR0 4YY

The paper and board used in this book are made from wood from responsible sources

Orchard Books
An imprint of Hachette Children's Group
Part of The Watts Publishing Group Limited
Carmelite House, 50 Victoria Embankment, London EC4Y 0DZ

An Hachette UK Company
www.hachette.co.uk
www.hachettechildrens.co.uk

To all the humans who've ever wondered what it would be like to be a pony

Contents

✴ ✴ ✴

CHAPTER 1

The Princess Summit

The castle of the Crystal Empire sparkled brilliantly in the midday sun. Ponies pranced around the Kingdom, running their daily errands in the market or playing outside in the gorgeous weather. In fact, everypony was so busy that they didn't notice that seven visitors from afar had just arrived through the front gate. It was six ponies and one small dragon, to be exact.

The recently crowned Princess Twilight Sparkle trotted along with her friends, pulling her suitcase behind her and taking in the dazzling scene. She loved visiting her brother's kingdom – this must have been her fourth or fifth visit so far! But for once, it wasn't because somepony needed saving!

This time, Twilight was here for another reason, and of course, her best friends had insisted on being there to support her. OK, and maybe to sample a few Crystal berry tarts or check out the Equestria Games stadium if there was time. Either way, it was comforting to have her best ponies there with her.

"Whoo-ee! Your very first Princess Summit. You must be over the moon, Twilight!" exclaimed Applejack, turning to her royal friend. Twilight Sparkle had taken up the lead, as royal p[...]

known to do. Twilight furrow[...]

in concern and looked back at her cr[...]

"Well, I *am* excited. But, to be honest..." Twilight stalled, then admitted, "I'm a little nervous, too." Twilight hadn't been a princess for very long, after all. Even after everything she'd learned from Princess Cadance and the Crystal Heart Spell, she still felt that there was much more to discover every day. Twilight just hoped she would have *something* to contribute to the Princess Summit.

Pinkie Pie trotted up to join them, a wide smile on her face and an extra bounce in her prance. "You're just *nervicited*!" Her curly fuchsia mane bounced wildly as she spoke. "It's like you want to jump up and down and yell, 'Yay me!'" She took a soaring leap into the air.

A ray of sunlight glinted against her pearly white smile. All of a sudden, she became serious and her face fell. "But you also want to curl up in a teeny-tiny ball and hide at the same time!" Pinkie fell to the ground and curled herself up, rocking back and forth.

Rarity and Rainbow Dash exchanged a sceptical look at the dramatic display before Pinkie Pie popped back up and patted Twilight reassuringly. "Don't worry, Twilight. We've all been there," Pinkie said knowingly.

Fluttershy, who had floated into the air for a moment to stretch her pale yellow wings, landed gracefully on the ground. "I'm there almost every day," she agreed in her soft voice. Up front, Twilight Sparkle took in her surroundings with just the slightest trace of hesitation. Even though she had visited the Empire several times before, the first glimpse of the Crystal Castle always stirred something inside her. It was just so big and beautiful. And intimidating. She took a deep breath and kept walking.

Applejack, who was trotting right beside her, noticed Twilight's frown. She was just about to toss a few more comforting words the princess's way when Rarity gasped in shock, stopping all six ponies in their tracks. "Sorry, darlings, but I just noticed that Twilight's not wearing her crown!" Rarity was always amazed that Twilight still felt self-conscious about wearing it.

"Don't worry, Rarity," Twilight assured her. "It's safe here in my bag."

"But you're attending a Princess Summit! I'm telling you, if I had a gorgeous crown like that I'd never take it off!" Rarity exclaimed. "Why, I'd sleep in the thing."

As soon as Twilight entered the hallway of the Crystal Castle, her nerves began to melt away like ice cream on a warm summer day. The Empire was starting to feel a little more like a home away from home to her. Twilight attempted to hold her head high in order to give off an air of confidence to anypony who might be watching, but the sound of royal trumpets suddenly blared through the castle. Twilight was startled by the loud racket and stumbled. Unfortunately, being a princess didn't automatically make a pony graceful.

"Ooof!" Twilight grunted as she braced herself on the chest of a handsome Crystal Royal Guard with a bright blue mane. He leaned forward to help her regain her balance with a small smile on his face. Then he remembered his duty and immediately snapped back to attention in time to announce her arrival.

"Her Highness, Princess Twilight Sparkle!" he projected his voice into the echoey Crystal corridor. Twilight blushed a little more than usual, though she didn't know why. It's not like she even knew this particular royal guard pony.

Nearby, Pinkie smiled wide with delight at all the pomp and circumstance. It just so happened that she loved pomp and also circumstance. But *together* – they were super-duper fun!

Suddenly, Princess Cadance, Princess Luna and Princess Celestia delicately trotted up to meet the six ponies and Spike. The ponies of the Crystal Royal Guard straightened themselves up to appear even taller than before.

Cadance smiled warmly. Her pink-and-purple mane cascaded into soft waves around her face, and she wore her own shimmering golden tiara so confidently, it seemed like it was a part of her. Maybe someday Twilight would, too. "Twilight! It's been so long since I've seen you!" Cadance nuzzled her young sister-in-law.

Princess Celestia stepped forward to join them, looking just as elegant and regal as the young princesses. Her pastel mane and tail flowed behind her. "We have so much to discuss. But it can wait until tomorrow. You all look tired from your journey." A quick glance at the pack of weary travellers was enough to confirm that she was right. Applejack, Rainbow Dash and Fluttershy all had dark circles forming under their eyes. Rarity's mane was looking a bit frizzy. And Pinkie Pie was twitching a little bit. But that could have been from excitement – it was hard to tell with her.

The ponies nodded in agreement and happily accepted Celestia's invitation to make their way to the guest quarters of the castle. As they hoofed their way down the hallway, their eyelids drooped with the heavy weight of sleep. Rarity was the only pony who remained alert – but that was just because she couldn't help but stare at every jewel and crystal encrusted in the archways and window frames. It was the type of decor she'd always envisioned herself living with.

It was really too bad that the friends were all too sleepy to notice that somepony was nearby. Somepony who was hiding in the shadows and watching their every move. Somepony who wanted to remain hidden.

Being the pony she was, Twilight couldn't go to sleep until all her belongings were unpacked and stowed away safely in the appropriate places. There had to be a certain order to things, whether she was at home in Ponyville or not. Routines helped her to feel like the same old Twilight she'd always been. Twilight's purple Unicorn horn glowed as she used her magic to put each item from her suitcase folded in a drawer, hung in the wardrobe, or placed on the bookshelf. (She'd only packed a couple of books.) Spike watched with mild interest, his attention being tested by the abundance of jewels everywhere. His gem-hoarding dragon instincts were starting to take over.

Twilight lifted the princess crown from her bag and tried to position it on her head. The delicate gold tiara supported a shimmering magenta gemstone – an Element of Harmony, a very powerful stone infused with Magic. But instead of looking pretty like Cadance's, the shining tiara dipped awkwardly down on one side, squashing Twilight's fringe. One look at her reflection confirmed Twilight's anxieties. She was no princess, and here she was at the Princess Summit! A summit of princesses!

"What's wrong, Twilight Sparkle?" asked Spike, suddenly snapping out of his daydream about a peanut butter and *jewelly* sandwich.

The crown slipped a little further down Twilight's face. It was no use. It floated up off her head as she used her horn to magically put it down gently on a table. "I'm just…worried, I guess. Princess Cadance was given the Crystal Empire to rule over. What if now that I'm a princess, Celestia expects me to lead a kingdom of my own?" Twilight stared at the crown, sitting lonely on a small, ornate table by her bed.

Spike marvelled at the idea of *his* Twilight running a kingdom. Maybe she'd make him into some royal advisor or better yet – jewel guard. "That. Would. Be. Awesome."

Twilight frowned. "No. It wouldn't!" She began to pace around. "Just because I have this crown and these new wings, it doesn't mean I'll be a good leader."

"Sure, you will," Spike said, using his last ounce of energy to cheer up his best friend. A wave of exhaustion washed over him. "Now come on. You should get some sleep. Big day tomorrow!" And with that, he crawled into the tiny bed that was set up next to Twilight's and made himself snug in his blanket. A short moment later, he was fast asleep, sucking on his claw.

It wasn't so easy for the new princess, however. She was absolutely desperate to find a comfortable position in which to rest her new wings. For the next ten minutes, she squirmed and stretched. She rolled and reached. She wiggled and wormed. Twilight had never realised how much work the feathery things could be! As she twisted around in her bed, Twilight made a mental note to discuss optimal wing-sleeping positions with Fluttershy and Rainbow Dash in the morning. Finally, she found a good spot. *That's better*, she thought, closing her eyes at last.

Sproing! Suddenly, her left wing popped out of the covers. Twilight sighed heavily. Apparently, there were a lot of things about her new life that were going to take some getting used to – summits, wings and crowns were only the start. But, hey, at least she didn't have to sleep in her crown.

Chapter 2

Sunset Shimmer Strikes at Night

Once all the little ponies were safely asleep in their plush Crystal rooms, the castle became shrouded in stillness – the kind that only happens in the middle of the night. In the daytime, the castle was filled with light and reflections that danced with one another, creating rainbow prisms on everypony who walked through its halls. But now every corner was met with a soft, eerie glow from the giant crescent-shaped moon. It flooded in through the glass windows and gave the whole place a super-spooky feeling.

Luckily for the red-and-golden-maned Unicorn who now crept through the corridor, it was easy to hide in the shadows. She was careful to tread lightly on her hooves. Any sudden noise could wake just one pony – or dragon – and ruin her entire mission. That yellow-and-pink Pegasus looked like an especially light snoozer. The last thing she needed was some scaredy-pony causing a stir and messing everything up. No – this was far too important a task to risk messing up.

It wasn't long before she found just the room she was looking for. The quarters of the newly "royal" Twilight Sparkle. Now if only she could get past that sleeping baby dragon and the princess herself...then everything she had ever wanted was within reach of her own little hooves. And a mere few minutes' time.

She pushed the heavy door, and it creaked open with little resistance. The room was illuminated by the moonlight, just like the castle corridor. She quickly took stock of the sleeping forms of both the princess and the dragon. It was no easy task to maintain her silence as she crept toward the bedside table. Towards her *true* destiny.

The red-and-golden-maned pony used her magic to levitate the very object of her desire and move it over to her. It looked even more beautiful up close. Twilight Sparkle's glittering crown was going to be hers.

The job was almost done when, suddenly, the baby dragon rolled over, mumbling. The Unicorn froze. She needed to be even more careful than she thought! That was a close one. *Too* close.

She stayed still until a loud snore came from the dragon's direction. It was the signal she needed to complete the deed. A wicked look flashed across her sweet golden face. Her next move was swift. She gently placed an identical replica of the royal crown in place of the original and sneaked back towards the door.

But just as the Unicorn tried to step over the restless dragon, her hoof became caught in one of his arms. She immediately lost her balance and crashed to the floor, causing both the dragon and the princess to wake with a jolt!

"Huh? What?" Spike said, rubbing his eyes sleepily.

The golden Unicorn scrambled to her

hooves in a panic. As she galloped towards the door, she stole a glance back at the confused princess. A ray of moonlight shone onto the mysterious pony and glinted off the stolen item that she was shoving in her bag. Twilight sucked in her breath in pure shock.

"My crown! She's got my crown!" she cried into the night. Twilight jumped into action and leaped out of bed, Spike following close behind. As she chased the thief down the hall, Twilight was filled with a sense of dread. What would happen if she couldn't catch that pony? She shouldn't have been so careless and left the precious crown out like that! What would Celestia say? Twilight knew she wasn't fit to be a princess yet, if ever. She just *had* to catch that Unicorn or risk everypony finding out how truly unroyal she was.

As she gained ground, running as fast as her hooves would carry her down the hallway, Twilight got a better look at the thief. The pony in question had a mane the colours of fire and a cutie mark to match. It was in the shape of a sun. Twilight didn't recognise her at all, but that didn't mean much. She had met so many new ponies since the coronation that sometimes it was difficult to keep track of them all.

"Stop! Thief!" Twilight shouted in desperation into the darkness. The commotion must have woken everypony in the castle, because doors on either side of the hallway started to burst open. Applejack, Rarity, Fluttershy, Rainbow Dash and Pinkie Pie all emerged from their respective rooms, looking sleepy.

"She's stolen my crown!" Twilight yelled

as she sped past them, with Spike two steps behind. The ponies barely had time to register what she'd said. They dutifully took off in the direction of the thief as well, hoping that they could help. Their friend was in trouble!

Twilight didn't understand where this Unicorn was going. The golden pony turned and galloped through the corridors without any hesitation whatsoever. She obviously knew her way around the castle and had a specific destination in mind. Maybe there was a secret exit? Or a hiding place?

Twilight kept up her speed, hoping at the very least that a member of the Crystal Royal Guard would soon step in. But a moment later, Twilight saw that there was no need for that. The Unicorn burst through the double doors of the last room at the end of the hall, and Twilight knew that this was it. The Unicorn was cornered. In fact, she was *unicornered*!

"Stop!" Twilight shouted as she entered the room, her friends coming up close behind her. "You have nowhere to run."

The Unicorn's face turned to panic as she realised there were now six ponies and one dragon against her. She clambered up onto the windowsill, looking back at her pursuers. The Unicorn faltered, tripping over her own hooves.

Her face fell as the bag with the crown inside flew through the air. The precious Element of Harmony was headed straight for a massive mirror. Everypony watched, completely frozen in place. But instead of crashing into the glass as they expected it to, the bag disappeared the moment it made contact with the mirror. It was just...gone!

Applejack gasped. "How did that—?"

"What did you do with my crown?!" Twilight exclaimed, thoroughly confused.

The golden Unicorn stood up and smirked wickedly at all the stunned Ponyville ponies.

"Sorry it had to be this way, *Princess*," the thief sneered before diving through the mirror herself. The ponies turned to one another in shock. A pony walking through a solid object? They'd seen a lot of unbelievable things in Equestria, but nothing like this.

Finally, Fluttershy broke the silence. "Who *was* that?" she whispered. It was what they were all thinking. But it was a question that nopony knew the answer to.

CHAPTER 3

A Royal Predicament

The Ponyville ponies had no choice but to wake the princesses and alert them to the recent events, even if it was the middle of the night. Not long after, an emergency meeting commenced in the throne room of the castle. Princess Cadance sat on her throne, Celestia and Luna flanking her. Celestia wore a solemn expression as she faced everyone in the room.

"Sunset Shimmer," Celestia said as

soon as she'd heard the description of the thief. "A former student of mine."

Rarity and Rainbow Dash raised their eyebrows at each other. They'd never even heard of her.

"She began her studies with me not long before Twilight," Celestia explained.

Twilight racked her brain and realised she did recall seeing the pony *somewhere* before. "I didn't really know her. But now I think I remember seeing her in Canterlot..."

"You would have." Princess Celestia nodded. "She was one of my most ambitious students. But when she did not get what she wanted as quickly as she liked, she became cruel and dishonest."

Twilight stepped forward, eager to hear more about the mysterious Unicorn-turned-thief.

Celestia lowered her head in defeat.

"I tried to help her, but she eventually decided to abandon her studies and pursue her own path. One that has sadly led her to stealing your crown."

Twilight tried to imagine taking such a terrible path. She couldn't dream up any reason that would make her act like Sunset Shimmer had that evening.

Spike stepped forward, grasping the fake crown in his claws. "She replaced Twilight's crown with this one."

Princess Celestia inspected the impostor tiara. It was very similar to Twilight's indeed. Shaking her head, she turned to Twilight.

"I suppose Sunset Shimmer thought you wouldn't notice right away that this was not yours. And by the time you did, it would be too late to go after your crown and the Element of Harmony that adorns it." Celestia sighed, clearly troubled by the situation at hoof.

Even after everything Celestia had explained, there were still so many questions that remained unanswered. The crown had disappeared into a mirror, and Sunset Shimmer had gone right in after it. That part made no sense at all.

"But I don't understand," Twilight piped up. "Where did she go? Where did she take the crown?"

Princess Luna and Princess Cadance, who had kept quiet through all this, exchanged a look of concern. They didn't say anything.

"You'll soon know more about this place than even I do," Celestia replied, looking dreamily off into the distance. Her mind was somewhere else. Somewhere mysterious. Somewhere that a golden

Unicorn and a missing crown probably were. And Twilight had a sneaking suspicion that she was about to go there, too.

Twilight's stomach was a ball of nerves. First, she'd got herself so worked up about the Princess Summit, and now she was about to visit a strange, unknown place to retrieve her irreplaceable Element of Harmony? It was almost too much to handle. But Twilight tried to remain brave. Brave like Princess Luna, who was now trying to explain the mysterious magic mirror in the corner of the room where they'd last seen Sunset Shimmer.

The ponies and Spike all gathered around Luna. The dark princess of the night looked especially regal in the moonlight. Her starry-blue mane sparkled, and the dark midnight hue of her coat looked extra shiny.

"This is no ordinary mirror," she explained. She pointed her hoof at the glass surface without touching it. "It is a gateway to another world."

Everyone's eyes grew wide with intrigue – except for Pinkie Pie's. Pinkie's eyes had already been wide before Luna began speaking.

Princess Luna looked directly at Twilight. "It's a gateway that opens only once every thirty moons."

"Oooooooohh. Sparkly," Pinkie Pie cooed. She leaned in a little bit closer and reached her hoof out to try and touch the surface of the mirror. Luna shook her head as a warning, and Pinkie pulled her hoof back, pouting at being stopped.

Luna explained that the mirror was usually kept in Canterlot Castle but had recently been brought to Princess Cadance in the Crystal Empire for safekeeping. Apparently, only a few nights before, Cadance had observed signs that the portal was opening again.

Princess Celestia looked into the mirror with a trace of sadness in her eyes. Twilight had never seen her this way. Celestia looked as if she were learning a hard lesson, even though she was usually the one doing the teaching. "I had always hoped that Sunset Shimmer would someday use it to return. To come back to Equestria seeking my guidance." She lowered her head.

"Twilight," Princess Cadance cut in, "you must use the mirror to go into this other world and retrieve your crown. Without it, the other Elements of Harmony have no power and Equestria is left without one of its most important means of defence." Cadance looked Twilight straight in the eye.

Twilight nodded. She knew that Cadance was right. The Elements of Harmony had protected Equestria on more than one occasion. Without her crown, everypony back home in Ponyville and everypony else in the Kingdom was left completely vulnerable. What if Queen Chrysalis somehow came back again? Or King Sombra? Or somepony even worse? It was a horrible thought.

It was as if Princess Luna were reading Twilight's mind. "In her possession, your Element of Harmony will no doubt be used to bring harm to the inhabitants of the realm that Sunset Shimmer now calls home," explained Luna. "They will not have the power to defend themselves."

Twilight didn't want to think about it too much, but she was starting to understand just how important her mission was to everypony. If the other princesses trusted her to do it, then there was no way she was going to let them down.

Celestia stepped forward. "You must go at once."

The young princess swallowed hard and nodded in agreement. But before she could step any closer to the mirror, Rainbow Dash blocked her path.

"Whoa, whoa, whoa!" Rainbow said, holding up her hooves in protest. "Strange new world. Crazy former student wants to use an Element of Harmony for evil…"

Rainbow cocked her head to the side. "…and you wanna send her there alone?"

Rainbow puffed up her chest and looked back to the Ponyville ponies for backup. "If she's going, we're going with her! Right, girls?"

Applejack stepped up to meet her, nodding. Rarity, Pinkie Pie and Fluttershy joined in as well. The only pony who looked happy about it, though, was Pinkie. She grinned, inspecting the shimmery glass once more. Twilight felt a bit safer knowing her friends would be by her side.

"I'm so nervicited!" Pinkie said to Applejack, who must have been a little less thrilled with the idea of going through the portal.

"You do know that's not a real word, right?" she retorted at the pink pony. But Pinkie ignored the statement and continued to grin at the mirror.

"I'm afraid I can't let you all go," Princess Celestia said to Rainbow Dash, who looked annoyed at being told what to do. "It would upset the balance of this alternate world, making it impossible for Twilight to get the crown back from Sunset Shimmer."

Celestia turned to her faithful student. "This is something Princess Twilight must do alone."

It was time. Twilight knew that she had to leave now, or risk losing her crown for ever. She looked to each of her friends, who had begun to gather around her. It was going to be so scary to go to a new world without them.

"You can do this, Twilight," encouraged Applejack, giving her a hug.

"You'll be back before you know it,"

added Fluttershy, giving a little smile.

"Time is of the essence!" Princess Luna interrupted the goodbyes, eager to see Twilight off on her quest. She placed a bag on Twilight's back, presumably for hiding the crown once it was recovered from Sunset Shimmer. Luna's face was serious as she spoke. "Remember, on the third day, when the moon reaches its peak in the night sky, the gateway will close. Once it does, it will be another thirty moons before you will be able to use it to return."

Rainbow Dash and Rarity looked to each other in concern. Three days wasn't much time at all.

Just when Twilight was about to step through the swirling mirror, Princess Celestia gave one final warning. "Twilight, things will look very different where you are going. Even *you* will look different."

Twilight wondered if maybe her wings would disappear again, then brushed the thought away. She really had no idea what to expect of this new world. Wings were the least of her problems right now.

"But if you use what you have learned here in Equestria," Celestia continued, "I am sure you will prevail."

"I'll do my best," Twilight replied sincerely. And with one final glance back at her friends, Twilight took a step through the filigreed arch of the shimmering frame.

CHAPTER 4

Through the Portal

In the last moment before she left the Crystal mirror room, Twilight thought she heard the ponies screaming Spike's name. But now that she was tumbling through the air, twisting and flipping through some unknown vortex, it was hard to tell. She couldn't focus on anything, let alone figure out what had happened to him. *Ouch!* Twilight thought as her body contorted and stretched. She couldn't see much. Just flashes of light, colours and a blurry green-and-purple thing…

"Spike!" Twilight tried to yell, but nothing happened. He tumbled alongside her, squishing and stretching. But maybe she was dreaming and he wasn't really there at all. *FLASH!* A white light flooded Twilight's vision.

Twilight blinked. Spiky green things everywhere. *Grass.* It was just grass!

She felt a bit like she'd fallen from the top spire of Canterlot Castle. In fact, her whole body was sore. It was probably some after-effects from the bumpy ride through the portal. Twilight leaned up and took in her surroundings. Green grass. Blue sky. A marble statue of a pony rearing up on its hind legs, in front of a massive red castle. So far, the strange new world seemed pretty much like Equestria.

Twilight noticed that the base of the statue looked shiny. It was almost as if it were made from the same mirrored material as the portal back in the Crystal Empire. Judging on where she was now sitting, it was a good bet that this was the other end of it! *Three days*, she reminded herself. *Or thirty more moons.*

"Uh…Twilight…" Spike's voice was coming from somewhere. So he *was* here after all. The little stowaway!

"Spike, you're not supposed to—" Twilight scolded, looking around for her dragon companion. Twilight gasped when she saw the creature next to her. It wasn't a dragon at all!

"Spike? Are you a … *dog*?" Twilight said to the little purple mutt wearing a spiked collar. His tail wagged involuntarily.

"I think so," the dog version of Spike

replied. He scrunched up his face. "But I have no idea what *you* are."

Before Twilight could ask him what he meant, she reached out her hoof to prop herself up. Only it wasn't a hoof!

"Aaaaaaaaaaaaaaaaaaaahhh!" Twilight screamed, looking at the things on the ends of her limbs. They were flat and had five sticks extending out from each of them. She wiggled them back and forth. They worked! Were these . . . "hands"? She had read about them somewhere before.

Twilight brought her new hands to her face to muffle her cries. She needed to get it together. If her hooves looked like this she couldn't imagine what the rest of her body looked like. She looked down at her torso. She was wearing a light blue shirt and a poufy purple skirt. On the left side of her skirt, a picture of her cutie mark – a

large pink star with five little white stars –
was stitched into the material! Interesting.

"You look like you. Only not you. Your
muzzle is really small," Spike observed,
trying to calm her down.

Twilight reached up and touched her
face. He was right – her muzzle had
completely shrunk down, and now she only
had a small nose, high up on her face. What
sort of dark magic was this? Twilight needed
to find the crown and get back to normal as
fast as possible. This was just *too* weird.

"Are you going to scream again?" asked
Spike, looking a little too amused for
Twilight's liking. She shook her head. It
was time to focus.

"So, I don't know where we are," she
said. "But that must be the gateway back
to Equestria." She pointed to the base of
the statue. "We need to get back here as

soon as we find the crown. I suggest we start searching the castle first."

Twilight stood up on all fours and tried to trot towards the castle. It was really hard to do with these new hooves. She felt like a foal learning to walk. It must have looked really odd, too, because Spike was giving her a funny look.

"Yeah, I don't think that's how the new you is supposed to…" Spike tried not to laugh. He was enjoying this a little too much. He pointed out a two-legged creature nearby, walking a dog like him on a leash. "See? I walk on all fours, while you walk on two," he said.

Twilight leaned back on her hind legs. This actually felt a little more comfortable. Twilight took several steps forward on just two legs. She started to move across the grass with ease. How peculiar.

Thinking back to the night before, Twilight couldn't believe she'd been worrying so much about just *wings*. Now she was in a completely unknown realm, stuck in a strange body that she didn't even know how to work! The sooner she found the crown, the better. Twilight did not want to be this weird creature for longer than she had to.

As she hobbled up to the castle entrance, she observed the large main doors. This castle, with its many windows and golden spires, looked very important. It was probably locked. She knew what she had to do. Twilight lowered her head to use her horn to magic the doors open. It was a really simple spell, but nothing happened. Her magic wasn't working! Celestia hadn't mentioned that part!

Spike joined her at the top of the stairs.

"Uh, Twilight? I hate to tell you this, but you don't exactly have your Unicorn horn any more."

CHAPTER 5

Storming the Castle

Once she'd got over the initial shock of being completely hornless, Twilight realised that the main doors had been unlocked all along! She just needed to give them a push. She and Spike entered the castle, careful to avoid being seen by any royal guards. This kingdom and everything about it was mysterious – there was no way Twilight was risking being thrown in a dungeon and trapped for thirty moons. Not in this body!

Twilight and Spike approached a glass case just inside the main entrance. Twilight tried to ignore the reflection of herself that she could now see. Her face was flat, and her body was tall and thin. What in Equestria *was* she? She shuddered and turned her attention back to the mission.

The case in front of them appeared to be protecting a bunch of golden relics. Most of them were shaped like goblets with elaborate handles. Some of them had names engraved into them, and others just said CHS. Twilight didn't see the crown in the case. That would be far too easy.

"What do you think, Spike?" Twilight said, looking for clues. "Are these other artifacts that Sunset Shimmer has stolen from Equestria?"

"Checking out my trophies, huh?" The sound of Rainbow Dash's voice made Twilight jump. She turned around and was met with the sight of one of her best friends. Well, sort of.

She still looked like the same old Rainbow Dash in a way – sporting a multi-coloured mane, a light blue hide and a smug expression. The only difference was that this Rainbow Dash had a strange body just like Twilight's new one. She was even wearing a cool outfit consisting of a red skirt, tall blue sneakers and a cobalt-blue shirt. Rarity would have approved of the sporty look.

"Rainbow Dash?" Twilight asked, unsure.

"The one and only!" Rainbow replied, with a familiar little smirk on her funny short-muzzled face.

"What are you doing here?" Twilight asked. Rule breaking always made Twilight uneasy. Apparently, even in this realm. But unlike Twilight, it wouldn't be the first time Rainbow had broken the rules. "Princess Celestia said I was the only one who could be here," Twilight scolded. Twilight was still trying to figure out how both Spike and Rainbow Dash had managed to jump in through the portal after her.

"*Princess* Celestia?" Rainbow looked at Twilight like she was completely nuts. "You mean *Principal* Celestia?"

"I…well…I don't…" Twilight stammered, trying to make sense of what that word even meant. Maybe *principal* was some sort of new nickname for *princess* that she hadn't heard yet. She raised an eyebrow at the bizarre version of Rainbow.

"I'm totally allowed to be here. I've got a hall pass," Rainbow retorted, holding up a small wooden paddle. She gave Twilight a sideways look. "Better run. Catch you later, new girl!"

As she watched Rainbow run off on her two hind legs, Twilight marvelled at the similarities between the new Rainbow and the old one. Everything she said and did seemed just like pony Rainbow Dash – but she obviously had no clue who Twilight was. It was fascinating.

BRIIIIING! Bells began to ring from every direction. Twilight and Spike stiffened, worried that they had somehow set off some sort of magic castle alarm. But before they could hide themselves, hundreds more creatures like Twilight – girls and boys – poured into the hallway through every door in sight. It was more crowded than the farm on Apple Day!

The creatures shuffled back and forth down the corridor, shoving into one another carelessly. They were all in such a rush. Twilight swayed back and forth, fighting to stay standing on her new legs amid all the commotion. She was still a little wobbly.

A sudden push from a girl with light purple hair (who strangely resembled Diamond Tiara from back in Ponyville) sent Twilight stumbling directly into someone else. Twilight soon lost control and continued to ping-pong through the bodies until a helpful arm reached out to break her fall.

"You OK?" the blue-haired boy creature said through a concerned expression. It was all she could do to nod a response and back away from him. This was the busiest castle she'd ever seen. Twilight was completely overwhelmed.

As if he'd read her mind, Spike whispered, "I don't think this is a castle." As she watched the girls and boys all around her – talking, laughing, and slamming tiny metal doors on the wall – Twilight silently agreed that the dragon-turned-dog might just be right. But if it wasn't a castle, then why did it need a crown?

The hallway crowd was starting to thin out, so Twilight didn't feel as panicky. She had been so busy getting used to this strange realm with its two-legged animals, she was wasting precious crown-finding time. She took a couple of deep breaths and tried to determine her next move. Twilight surveyed the area with caution, peeping in all directions like a spy. Spike just shrugged and thumped his new tail.

"I'm really sorry," whimpered a tiny voice from around the corner. "I just found it and thought I should give it to her." Twilight would know that soft voice anywhere – there was no doubt that it was Fluttershy! And she was in trouble.

Twilight leaned around a set of the green metal locking doors that lined the walls to get a better look. Sure enough, a girl with vibrant red-and-golden hair leaned over someone who was definitely this world's version of Fluttershy. Twilight recognised her friend immediately – her light pink mane and demure expression were unmistakable. "I didn't know that you dropped it," Fluttershy explained to the other figure, whose face was hidden.

"Well, I did and I was about to get it before you swooped in and ruined everything! You shouldn't just pick up things that don't belong to you," she growled. Whatever this other two-legged person had dropped must have been really important for her to be so mean to someone else.

"It really doesn't belong to you, either," Fluttershy squeaked.

"You really are pathetic, Fluttershy. It's no wonder your best friends are all stray animals."

Twilight couldn't bear to listen to her friend be treated like this. It was just so mean!

"How dare you speak to her that way!" Twilight interjected as she stepped into view. A hush fell over the hall, and everyone else stopped to watch the scene unfold. Apparently, standing up to her was a big deal or something.

The bully spun around. A look of anger flashed across her big green eyes. "What did you say?!" she bellowed, hooves on her hips. Well, not hooves, but…whatever.

Now that Twilight got a better look, she could see the bully was very fashionable. Her short orange skirt and black leather jacket made her look tough and showed some attitude. The girl crossed her arms defensively and took a few slow steps closer to Twilight.

"I *said*—" Twilight stepped forward, too, "how *dare* you speak to her that way!"

"You must be new here," the red-and-golden-haired two-leg sneered. Her eyes darted around at the small audience that had gathered to gawk at Twilight's bold move. "I can speak to *any*one *any* way I want!" she shouted, shoving Twilight out of the way and storming down the corridor.

A dozen whispered conversations erupted in every direction. Surely, everyone was wondering who Twilight was and where she had come from.

Fluttershy smoothed down her light green skirt and took a deep breath, trying to calm her nerves. "I can't believe that you stood up to Sunset Shimmer! Nobody ever does," she cooed, looking at Twilight as if she were some sort of hero, like the Mare Do Well of Ponyville. "Everyone is afraid of that girl."

"Sunset Shimmer?!" Twilight shouted. Now that's why the bully seemed so familiar. It was just the pony – er, *girl*, she was looking for. Twilight smiled. It wouldn't be long before she and Spike would retrieve the crown and head straight back to Equestria. Totally easy!

"You've heard of her?" Fluttershy

pushed a lock of her shiny pink hair behind her ear. It drew attention to her butterfly-shaped hairclip. It looked exactly like the real Fluttershy's cutie mark. "I don't think I've seen you around before. Did you just transfer to Canterlot High from another school?"

So that's what this building was supposed to be! "Um, yes. Another... school," Twilight replied. This sure was an odd-looking school, but that definitely made more sense than a castle. "My name's Twilight," she said with a smile.

"I'm Fluttershy," Fluttershy whispered, barely audible. "And, oh my goodness, who's this sweet little guy?" Fluttershy bent down to give Spike a pat on the head. Then she unzipped her bag and pulled out a treat. Spike wagged his tail and wolfed it down right away.

"That's Spike! My...dog," Twilight Sparkle said.

"He's so cute." Fluttershy grinned at the pup. Spike looked up at Fluttershy appreciatively and tried to make a convincing barking sound. Twilight suppressed a laugh.

"So, Fluttershy, Sunset Shimmer said you picked something up. Something that belonged to her," Twilight said. "It was a crown, wasn't it?"

Fluttershy's eyes widened. "How did you know?"

"Um, lucky guess?" Twilight offered. "Do you still have it?"

"No," Fluttershy whispered. "But I know what happened to it."

CHAPTER 6

Search for Celestia

"Oh, really?" Twilight said. She'd been listening patiently while Fluttershy told a lengthy story about how Canterlot's animal shelter was in trouble. Fluttershy was doing all she could to help them by trying to recruit new volunteers before and after school. So far, not many students had signed up. It was a sweet story, but Twilight was in a hurry. This was a royal emergency!

"So you were passing out flyers before school this morning and the crown just hit you in the head?" Twilight asked. It must have come through the portal at the base of the statue out front.

"I have no idea how it got there," Fluttershy explained, shaking her head. "But I didn't want anything to happen to it, so I decided I had to give it to Principal Celestia."

"She's the ruler here?" Twilight asked. Finally she was making some progress.

"I guess you could say that." Fluttershy shrugged. "Technically, I guess she and Vice Principal Luna do make the rules. Principal Celestia's office is the third door on the left, if you want to talk to her." Fluttershy pointed down the long hallway.

"Thank you!" Twilight replied, turning to leave. Spike followed dutifully.

"Oh, wait!" Fluttershy called out behind her. "You're not really supposed to have pets on school grounds. Might want to tuck him into your backpack. That's what I do." Fluttershy unzipped her bag to reveal a fuzzy bunny, a little bird, and a kitten, all cuddling one another. Twilight smiled. Same old Fluttershy!

Twilight hated to do it – but it was better to hide Spike in her bag than to risk drawing even *more* attention to herself. Twilight unzipped the backpack and bent down to Spike.

He was pouting. She just shrugged helplessly. He sighed. "Backpack it is…" he conceded as he jumped in.

As soon as Twilight entered Principal Celestia's office, she could tell she was on the right path. She'd always found comfort in Celestia's guidance back in Equestria.

This version – with her flowing pastel locks of blue, lavender, and green – seemed no different. She sat behind a desk, wearing a honey-coloured blazer, and was busy writing something. As usual, she seemed calm and put together. The perfect teacher. And now Twilight was a student again.

"How may I help you?" said Principal Celestia, gesturing for Twilight to make herself comfortable. Twilight was careful to set her bag down gently so as not to hurt Spike. She unzipped it a little so he could see.

"Um, uh…" Twilight stammered. "My name's Twilight. I'm new here and—"

Principal Celestia raised her eyebrows at Twilight inquisitively. It was probably better to just cut to the chase. Twilight continued. "I understand that Fluttershy found a crown this morning and gave it to you."

"Yes. Vice Principal Luna put it somewhere for safekeeping," Principal Celestia said, and smiled. "Why? Were you interested in running for princess of the Fall Formal this year?"

"Princess of the Fall Formal?" Twilight asked. She was about to tell Principal Celestia that the crown was actually hers, but this was intriguing. It seemed that they had princesses in this realm, too. And from the looks of things back in the hallway, it was possible that Sunset Shimmer was currently reigning.

"It's Canterlot High's big autumn dance!" Celestia explained. She motioned to a poster on the wall advertising the event. Pictures of blue balloons and mugs of fizzy drinks adorned the edges, along with all the details of the event. It looked just like the Grand Galloping Gala.

"We had something like it at my old... school," Twilight said, nodding.

"And was there a princess?" Celestia asked, her eyes warm.

"Yes, but she wasn't exactly a student." Twilight giggled. It was amusing to be explaining to *this* Celestia that there was a princess back in her Canterlot as well. Twilight, of course, left out the fact that it was a pony version of the principal herself.

Celestia nodded. "Here at Canterlot High, the students select one of their peers to represent them. She receives her crown at the Fall Formal."

Twilight was starting to get an idea. "Can anyone run for princess?"

"Yes, you just need to let the head of the Fall Formal Planning Committee know you'd like to be on the ballot," Principal Celestia said, but she seemed to sense that Twilight had lots of unspoken questions. "Was there anything else?"

"Um, no. That was it," Twilight lied. What was she supposed to say? *Hi, I'm actually a pony princess from another realm. Can I have the crown back right now, please and thank you?*

Princess Celestia smiled. "Well, if you need anything else, my door is always open."

Outside in the hallway, Spike popped his doggy head out of the bag. "Twilight, what are you doing?! Why didn't you just tell her the crown was yours and ask for it back?"

"What if she didn't believe me?" Twilight said.

She knew it was the right choice not to

mention the crown or Equestria to Principal Celestia. Based on her earlier interactions with Rainbow Dash, Fluttershy and Sunset Shimmer, it was clear that nobody here recognised her at all. And one thing was for sure – she would think anypony that came to Ponyville saying he or she was from a place filled with talking animals that walked on two legs was crazy.

"Looks like if I want my crown back, I'll have to become princess of the Canterlot High Fall Formal." Twilight lifted her chin decidedly. "So that's what I'm going to do."

After all, she'd already become a princess back in Equestria, right? How hard could it be? Except she only had a few days. Twilight looked to Spike. He seemed sceptical about this plan, but it was the only one she had.

Now if only she knew how she was ever going to accomplish it.

CHAPTER 7

A Lunchroom Divided

It didn't seem possible, but the Canterlot High cafeteria was even more crowded than the hallways. The massive room was packed. Tons of chattering students sat at the long white tables that were lined up in the centre of the room. Everyone was just hanging out and seemed to be having a great time.

Various school flags and posters hung high up on the walls, above the tall windows. Some of the signs said GO, CHS! and some had swirly gold writing that read WONDERCOLTS. The energy of the room reminded Twilight of a party in the big barn at Sweet Apple Acres, but a lot shinier. And a *lot* noisier.

Twilight watched the scene with mild curiosity while standing in the lunch line behind her new (and only) friend at school. It was still a little awkward using her "hands", so balancing her lunch tray was no small task. She followed close behind Fluttershy, hoping to blend in. It was working so far.

Fluttershy handed her tray to the lunch lady, who scooped a big glob of unidentified orange food onto her plate. When Twilight handed hers over, she nearly dropped it because the dinner lady looked so much like Applejack's grandmother Granny Smith. Chances were that it *was* Granny Smith, which made Twilight wonder whom else she might run into from back home.

But she wasn't here to socialise. Twilight was here on a mission.

"Fluttershy? I've decided to run for princess of the Fall Formal, and I was wondering if you might be able to help—"

At this, Fluttershy's jaw dropped and so did her fruit cup. Juice splattered everywhere, including all over Twilight's purple skirt. Fluttershy scrambled to look for a napkin. Luckily, Granny Smith threw her a tea towel.

"Oh, gosh. Sorry!" she whimpered. "It's just that running for Fall Formal princess is a really, really, really bad idea."

"Why?" asked Twilight, trying to dab some juice off her skirt.

"You seem really nice, and I really

appreciate you standing up for me earlier..." Fluttershy seemed hesitant to break the news. She looked around the cafeteria and lowered her voice. "But Sunset Shimmer wants to be Fall Formal princess. And when she wants something, she gets it."

The two girls took their trays to one of the long tables and sat down. "She'll make life miserable for anyone who stands in her way!" Fluttershy said. She took a tiny bite of the orange glop on her plate and made a face. It must have tasted pretty awful.

"Well, I have to try," said Twilight, determined.

Twilight appreciated Fluttershy's concern, but Fluttershy didn't really know what was at stake here for Equestria. There was no way she could have, seeing as she knew nothing about the pony world and its inhabitants.

"But you'd have to persuade all the groups to vote for you instead of her," explained Fluttershy. She motioned to the other tables, each one filled with a different category of students. Twilight soon learned that there were a bunch of different cliques at Canterlot High School. On one side of the cafeteria sat a table of athletes all tossing a ball to one another. Rainbow Dash was among them. Nearby, the fashionistas were all reading magazines and applying brightly coloured make-up. And next to *them* was the table Fluttershy called the "dramas" – they all seemed to be reading lines from some sort of play. The other side of the cafeteria had even more groups, including the eco kids, the techies and the rockers!

Twilight stared at the rocker table,

specifically at the blue-haired boy who'd helped her in the hallway. He was strumming a red electric guitar and looking out of the window dreamily. He looked kind of cute. *For a weird two-legged animal*, Twilight thought, smirking.

"Why is everypony – I mean, *everybody* separated this way?" Twilight pondered out loud.

Fluttershy sighed. "At CHS, everybody sticks to their own kind. The only thing they have in common is that they know Sunset Shimmer is going to rule this school until we graduate."

"Not if I can help it!" Twilight said. She leaned down to her tray and bit into an apple just as she would have back home in Ponyville. She didn't even realise she was still trying to eat like a pony until Fluttershy made a weird face. She was going to have to be more careful not to act like her old self from now on. Twilight wanted to impress the population of Canterlot High, not scare them!

Twilight removed the apple from her teeth and gave an embarrassed chuckle. "So, um, where would I find the head of the Party Planning Committee?"

After all, this was the only plan Twilight had. So she was sticking to it. Not even the horrified expression on Fluttershy's face could stop her.

Fluttershy had refused to come along, but luckily, it had been easy enough for Twilight and Spike to find the school gym from Fluttershy's directions. After they'd wandered through several halls that were lined with "lockers" and doors to classrooms, Twilight saw it. The piles of boxes outside the door labelled DANCE DECORATIONS hinted that they had found what – or *whom*, rather – they were looking for.

"Incoming!" shrieked a voice from across the Canterlot High gymnasium. Twilight and Spike ducked to narrowly avoid being hit in the head with a bright pink streamer that soared through the air. Streamers of sunshine yellow and sky blue soon followed, soaring through the rafters like some sort of party attack.

When it was all over, a girl with bright pink hair and a smile from ear to ear popped up. "Sorry about that. You really gotta chuck 'em if you want to get 'em up there!" She giggled. Judging by her wild mane of curly pink hair, her bubbly demeanour, and the picture of three balloons on her bright pink party skirt, Twilight had a pretty good idea of who this girl might be.

"Hi. My name's Twilight Sparkle and..." Twilight said, hoping to run through this introduction quickly. She was starting to get worried. The clock was ticking away.

"Oooh. Pretty name," the girl cooed. "I'm Pinkie Pie!"

"Somehow, I knew that," Twilight joked.

"Really? Are you psychic?!" Pinkie started to blow up a shiny blue balloon, then stopped suddenly. She eyed Twilight with suspicion. "Who is going to win *Canterlot Idol*? No, no. Don't tell me! But seriously, can you predict the future?!" It all spilled out faster than a kicked-over mug of fizzy apple juice.

"Uhh...I don't think so," Twilight said, unsure. Was that something they could do in this realm? "Fluttershy said this is where I'd find the head of the Fall Formal Planning Committee. I'm going to guess that's you."

Pinkie's face turned a little bit sour. "Fluttershy, huh? Don't let that whole shy thing fool you. She can be a real meanie."

Of all the things she'd seen and heard so far, this was the most surprising. Pinkie Pie and Fluttershy not getting along? Never in a million years would Twilight have expected that. "You two aren't friends?" she asked.

Pinkie let go of the balloon in her hand. It shot off, releasing its air in a pitiful loop before landing on the ground. "Not any more," Pinkie sighed.

She skipped over to a pile of colourful decorations in the corner and grabbed a neon-pink clipboard.

"Anyhoo, just need to fill this out and you are officially up for the coveted princess of the Fall Formal crown!" Pinkie said. "Even if you did wait a bit to get your name on the ballot. The dance is the day after tomorrow!"

Twilight awkwardly scrawled her name on the sheet, trying her best to use her "hand" things to write. Man, she missed her horn. Back in Ponyville, drafting up letters and spells was much easier. She secretly hoped no one would notice how bad her writing looked.

"Wow. You have *really* bad handwriting. It's like you never held a pen before." Pinkie Pie giggled at the idea.

Well, so much for that, thought Twilight.

"Someone order a dozen cases of fizzy apple juice?" A blonde girl wearing a brown cowgirl hat and boots walked into the gym, and a tall boy in a red shirt was trailing behind her. He was carrying a bunch of crates.

"Me! Me! Me!" Pinkie said, bouncing up and down. "Thanks, Applejack! Thanks, Big Mac!"

"Eeeeyup," said the boy version of Big Mac, before going out to grab more crates.

Applejack suddenly noticed Twilight's presence. "Hey! You're the new girl who gave Sunset Shimmer the what for in the hall today." Twilight wasn't sure if this was going to turn out to be a good thing or a bad thing.

Pinkie started to help Applejack unload bottles of fizzy apple juice, licking her lips at the sugary drink.

"I'm Twilight Sparkle," she said. "I'm going to run against Sunset Shimmer for princess of the Fall Formal."

"Who-ee, Sugarcube! I'd think twice about that. Watch out for the back stabbin'." Applejack shook her head then added, " 'Bout the only girl at this school you can trust less than Sunset Shimmer is Rainbow Dash."

"Rainbow Dash?" Twilight asked, getting more confused by the second.

"She's the captain of, like, every team at Canterlot High," Pinkie explained.

"She's also the captain of sayin' she's gonna do somethin' for you and then turnin' around and not even botherin' to show up!" Applejack crossed her arms across her chest in a huff.

First, Pinkie had put down Fluttershy, and now Applejack didn't trust Rainbow?

Why weren't any of her friends *friends*?! This place was bizarre and unsettling. Twilight was going to pry further, but something told her that all would reveal itself in the next few days. Maybe with a little help from some good old-fashioned research, or maybe Twilight was actually starting to become a little psychic. Either way, she had a lot of work to do if she wanted to win the crown.

CHAPTER 8

Sunset Comes After Twilight

A little while later, Twilight and Spike were across campus, walking outside in the sunshine and trying to figure out their next move.

"I can't believe I didn't recognise you earlier, *Twilight Sparkle*," Sunset Shimmer snapped, stopping Twilight and Spike in their tracks. Sunset continued on, sizing them up. "Pinkie Pie and Applejack told me everything. That is, after I made sure they knew what an *awful* job they were doing on my coronation decorations." Sunset flipped her fiery hair. "Honestly? Fizzy apple juice? It's not a hoedown!"

Twilight and Spike exchanged a sceptical look. Unlike all the other students at Canterlot High, they weren't scared of her.

"Should have known Princess Celestia would send her prize pupil here after my crown," Sunset laughed. "And her little dog, too."

Spike frowned.

"It's *my* crown," Twilight said, standing firm. "If you already rule this place, then why do you need it?"

"Pop quiz: what happens when you bring an Element of Harmony into an alternate world?" Sunset Shimmer sneered. She put her hands on her hips.

Twilight was drawing a serious blank. She should know this! The Elements of Harmony were mysterious, but she'd read every single bit of available literature on them. She'd memorised each page and even created new magic after the debacle where everypony's cutie marks had got switched. It was the reason why she was a princess to begin with!

"You don't know? And you're supposed to be Celestia's star student?" Sunset Shimmer guffawed. "Then again, what were the chances she'd find somepony as bright as me to take under her wing after I left Equestria?" Whatever she was, Sunset Shimmer certainly wasn't humble.

Twilight reeled with the knowledge that there was something about the Elements of Harmony that she didn't know, but Sunset Shimmer did. Why hadn't Celestia warned her? Unless she didn't know, either.

Sunset Shimmer walked all around Twilight, looking her up and down. "Bit embarrassing that you were the best she could do, though."

Spike began to growl. He almost sounded like a real dog.

Twilight looked down at herself. She *was* sort of a mess. Her purple skirt was still stained with fruit juice from lunch. Her arms were all scraped up from trying to trot like a pony through the sticks and grass out on the front lawn that morning. And on top of everything, she didn't even know what an Element of Harmony – her own crown – did in this realm.

"I'd keep an eye on your mutt. Canterlot High has a very strict 'no pets allowed' policy," Sunset Shimmer said

* * **88** * *

with a wicked smile. She pointed at Spike. "Hate for him to be taken away from you."

Spike couldn't keep quiet any longer. He stood upright and put his paws on his hips. "Is that a threat?"

"Of course not," Sunset Shimmer said, her voice dripping with sugary sweetness. "But I'd cut down on the chatter if I were you. Don't want everyone to know you two don't belong here, now would you?" And with that she turned on her heel and headed back towards the gym.

After about five steps, she turned around and looked at Twilight. "You want to become a princess here? Please. You'll never stand out! You don't even know the first thing about fitting in."

When Sunset Shimmer reached the doors, her two henchmen – Snips and Snails – tumbled out. "I want you to follow her," she snapped, now out of Twilight's earshot. "Bring me something I can use, just like you did with the last girl who thought she could challenge me."

Whenever Twilight was really stumped back in Equestria, there was always one place she knew she could go for guidance. One place where she felt like she could really understand things. One place that could certainly be found in any school. Even Canterlot High.

"I knew there'd be a library!" Twilight said as she stared up at the brick building in awe. A few students pushed through the doors, carrying large stacks of books. Finally, Twilight felt a little at ease in this realm. She skipped up the steps, Spike at her heels. "If I'm going to really fit in and win votes, we need to do some research." Twilight couldn't risk that Sunset Shimmer might just be right about her not knowing how to fit in. And apparently, it was a big deal at this high school.

"Research?" Spike said, groaning. He imagined having to help her put away all her books, just like at home in Ponyville.

Twilight pushed the big double doors open and stepped inside. It was gorgeous! A tall, domed ceiling arched over the circular room. Hundreds of books were stacked on shelves that stretched up two floors high. A golden bust of a Wondercolt shone in the centre of a workstation that was surrounded by black square things. They had flat boards full of buttons in front of them. Twilight had no idea what they were even for. Some sort of musical instrument, perhaps?

Nearby, a group of three younger girls sat in front of one of the black square things, giggling. It looked like they were watching something. "Maybe this place does have magic," Twilight mumbled to herself, marvelling at the moving images dancing across the front of the box.

A woman came up to the girls and shook her head. "Sorry, Apple Bloom. School computers are for research only. Please get back to class. You, too, Sweetie Belle and Scootaloo." The girls all groaned.

"It's just as well, y'all," said Apple Bloom. "Some of the comments about our music video were really awful." She had the same country twang in her voice as Applejack.

"Bye, Miss Cheerilee," the girls called

as they headed out of the library.

Twilight stared at the black thing quizzically. Maybe she could use one of those things for research. That's what Cheerilee had said they were for after all. Kind of like a book. Except not.

In a matter of minutes, Miss Cheerilee had set up Twilight with her own "computer".

"So I just push the letters here and then words and moving pictures will come up here?" asked Twilight, staring down at the strange device.

"That's right!" Miss Cheerilee nodded with a smile.

Twilight punched her hands into the keyboard. She accidentally applied way too much force and ended up jamming her fingers. "Ouch!" she cried. Having hands was hard. Spike raised an eyebrow.

Twilight was starting to cause a scene with her awkward antics. She shook her head at him, and he stayed quiet. So quiet, in fact, that he fell asleep.

Little did Twilight and Spike know, Snips and Snails were crouched behind a bookshelf filming Twilight with a mobile-phone camera the entire time. They sniggered at each other. "Sunset Shimmer is going to love this!" said Snips, rubbing his hands together in giddiness. Now all they had to do was wait for that wannabe Twilight Sparkle to do something else worth watching. Then she'd learn what happened to girls who messed with Sunset Shimmer.

"I know it's a little dusty." Spike coughed as he led Twilight up the stairs into a lofty room at the top of the library. "But it doesn't seem like anybody comes up here. I thought we could sleep here tonight."

Twilight stopped herself from mentioning that Spike had already had a nice long nap under the table in the library while she did research.

Twilight batted away a cobweb and sneezed. Dust billowed into the air.

"It's perfect, Spike," she said. "I can't believe I hadn't even thought about it. Too busy researching, I guess."

"How did it go?" Spike asked as he moved some old dusty books out of the way to make room.

"I found this." Twilight held up a large book that said CHS WONDERCOLTS across the front. "It's called a 'yearbook'. It seems to be something that they use to keep a record of things that have happened at the school." She flipped open the book and riffled through until she found a particular page. "Look!"

It was a picture of Pinkie Pie, Rainbow Dash, Applejack, Fluttershy and a girl with violet hair all embracing one another. They were smiling. "I'm going to bet the girl on the far right is Rarity."

"There's a Rarity here?!" Spike jumped up. His crush on Rarity back in Equestria was no secret to anypony. "I mean... interesting photo."

"It's interesting because they look like they're friends." Twilight wore an expression of distress. "But it doesn't seem like they are now."

"Not so much," Spike agreed. The way Pinkie had talked about Fluttershy being a "meanie" and Applejack had said she didn't trust Rainbow were both good clues to that. But there had to be some deeper reason that the girls' friendships had ended.

Twilight shook her head and sat down on the filthy floor. "I just can't help but get the feeling that Sunset Shimmer had something to do with it."

When Twilight went off on a tangent like this, it was often up to Spike to steer her back to her true goal. "But she wants your crown because she's planning on doing something even worse. If you're going to stop her, you have to focus on making allies here. You can't worry about why these girls aren't friends any more."

Spike was right. She needed to keep her eyes on the prize and not get sidetracked by the new girls she'd met here. Even if they did remind her of her Ponyville friends.

Twilight closed her eyes and burrowed down in the old books. She needed to get some rest for tomorrow. It was a big day. Tomorrow Twilight would earn the respect of *everyone* at Canterlot High. Well, everyone except for maybe one girl with golden hair.

CHAPTER 9

The Wrong Kind of Attention

The next morning, Twilight was ready with a plan. She had woken up in the middle of the night thinking about all the kids at Canterlot High.

"Fluttershy said I'd need to win over all those different groups if I want to become princess of the Fall Formal, so I've compiled a list of talking points," Twilight explained. First, she would introduce herself. Next she would sprinkle in some things she'd learned about this world into casual conversation. Maybe something about computers? Then they would decide she was really nice and want to vote for her for Fall Formal princess.

Spike ambled across the dewy grass on the front lawn next to her. "You made a list? That's so unlike you."

Twilight bent down to her dog and opened her backpack. "Come on, Spike. Time to make a good first impression on my fellow students. The whole world sort of depends on it."

Spike climbed in with a whimper. This hiding thing was already getting old.

Inside the school, Principal Celestia's voice boomed through some sort of magical announcement system as Twilight navigated her way through the bustling main halls. "Good morning, students, and happy Thursday! Just a reminder to pick up your ballots for the princess of the Fall Formal today. They are due by the time the dance starts tomorrow night, so don't forget to vote and make your voice heard."

Twilight smiled. She was actually getting sort of excited about the whole thing. She scanned the hallway for someone new to meet. There were lots of kids around, so it would be pretty easy. Twilight spotted a fashionista girl wearing a cute dress and pink knee-socks with sparkles in them. *Perfect.*

"Hi, I'm Twilight!" She waved to the girl. "Love your socks. Pink is definitely the new black." The girl gave Twilight a funny look before shuffling off to one of her friends. The two of them whispered something to each other, looked back at Twilight, and began to giggle.

That was weird.

"Hey there!" Twilight said to a burly guy in a blue Wondercolts football jersey. "Offence sells tickets, but defence wins games." She grinned. Surely her knowledge of the game "football" would help her to connect with him. But the boy didn't smile back. He just looked at his friends and then laughed. How rude!

Twilight looked around the hallway in confusion. It wasn't just the fashionista and football guy who were laughing at her. Almost all the students were giving her strange looks!

"Spike," Twilight whispered to her backpack. "Why is everybody looking at me funny?"

"Psssst!" a voice hissed from nowhere.

Suddenly, an arm adorned with a gold bangle bracelet reached out and yanked

Twilight into an empty classroom. Twilight now stood face-to-face with a pretty girl. She had dark purple hair and wore a diamanté hair clip. Her long eyelashes enhanced her worry-filled, big blue eyes.

"Rarity?" Twilight suddenly recognised the girl from the yearbook picture. She wore a lavender skirt with Rarity's cutie mark of three diamonds on it.

Rarity pulled out a wig and slapped it on Twilight's head. "Too poufy," Rarity winced. She pulled out another. "Too shiny!" she exclaimed.

"What are you doing?" Twilight said, yanking the shiny wig off her head. It was all hot and itchy. Besides, she liked her mane how it was – indigo with a few chunks of pink and plum running through it.

Rarity looked Twilight up and down like

she was some sort of project. "We need something that says, 'I am totally new here, and you have never seen me before.' Everyone's going to remember the purple and pink, darling, from the video." She riffled through her bag, which contained a ridiculous amount of extra clothes. She found a green dress and began to dress Twilight like a doll. "This is good! No one will recognise you."

"Why wouldn't I want to be—?" Twilight said, her voice muffled by the green fabric.

Rarity ignored Twilight's question and bent down to Spike, who had jumped out of his backpack prison. She gave him a little pat on the head, and his tail started wagging. "And we'll need a disguise for your *adorable* dog, too. With a little work, I think I could make him look like a rabbit."

Twilight was still trying to figure out why she even needed a disguise when Applejack burst into the room. "There you are, Twilight." Fluttershy and Pinkie Pie filed in after her.

"Oh, poo," huffed Rarity. She threw her arms up in defeat. "So much for the disguise."

"We've been lookin' all over for you," Applejack said.

"I like your new look, Twilight!" Pinkie Pie chirped.

Rarity scoffed. "Yes, well, I do have an eye for these sorts of things. Not that *you* seem to care."

The comment struck a chord in Twilight. As much as she tried not to care that these versions of her best friends weren't getting along, it really bothered her. She wanted to say something about it, but she held her tongue. A subject change was better. "So, why were you all looking for me? What's going on?"

By the looks on everyone's faces, she could tell that whatever it was, it was bad. Very, very bad.

The girls showed her the screen on Pinkie Pie's laptop and played a video. Twilight Sparkle gasped at what she saw. "But this all happened yesterday. At the library," she protested, genuinely stumped. "How did a video of me falling over and acting like a – I mean, me acting *strange* get on the computer?"

The video was awful. It included all the embarrassing things that had happened to Twilight, including when she dropped a stack of books and started picking them up with her mouth out of habit. At the end of the montage, Sunset Shimmer had come on-screen and urged everyone not to vote for Twilight for princess.

"Has everyone in the school seen this?" Twilight asked. So that explained all the weird glances and whispers. Geez, high school was really rough!

Rarity sighed. "She did the same thing to me when I tried to be princess of the Spring Fling. Had those *freshmen* – Snips and Snails – follow me to the boutique where I work after school. They filmed me pretending a mannequin was a prince and asking him for a…a…kiss!" Rarity started to blush crimson at the memory.

Applejack shook her head and crossed her arms. "I tried to tell you, Twilight."

Pinkie Pie jumped up. "Sunset Shimmer's got things all turned around! People are supposed to laugh *with* you, not at you. Duh."

Twilight slumped. "What am I going to do? No one is going to vote for me after seeing this."

"Not that it will make any difference, but I'd still vote for you." Fluttershy looked up from staring at her shoes. "You were so nice to me when Sunset Shimmer was picking on me yesterday."

Pinkie Pie walked over to Twilight and leaned on a desk. "If you still want to run, maybe there's something I can do to help."

Twilight was about to thank her when Fluttershy leaned in and made a big show of shielding her mouth. "Word of advice. Don't accept her help. She doesn't take anything seriously."

"Why do you have to be so awful to me?!" Pinkie whined.

"Don't play innocent," snapped Rarity. "You're no better than she is."

"Listen to y'all carryin' on. Get over it and move on!" Applejack chimed in.

Rarity scoffed. "You mean like how you've got over what happened with Rainbow Dash? The way she said she'd bring the netball team to your bake sale and then was a total no-show?"

This was more than Twilight could handle. All four girls were dishing insults at one another left and right. The ponies she knew back home would never talk to anyone like that. Especially not their friends.

"Stop! All of you!" Twilight yelled, bringing the bickering to a halt. "I want to show you something." Twilight dug through her backpack and found the yearbook. This was just what the girls needed to remind them of their friendship. "You were friends once."

Twilight pushed the book towards them.

Applejack was the first to crack. "The Freshman Fair," she said, a trace of longing in her voice. "Y'all remember?"

Twilight turned to face them. All four were staring at the picture, fighting the urge to smile at the memory. "But something happened. I think that something was Sunset Shimmer."

"Sunset Shimmer wasn't the one who ruined my silent auction for the animal shelter by bringing fireworks and noisemakers." Fluttershy pouted. "It was supposed to be a serious event, and Pinkie ruined it."

"What are you talking about?" Pinkie looked at Fluttershy like she was crazy. "I got a text message from *you* saying that you didn't want a silent auction, you wanted a big party!"

"I never sent you a text." Fluttershy blinked innocently.

Pinkie made a face. "You didn't?"

After they cleared up that misunderstanding, it soon came out that Pinkie Pie and Rarity had been similarly tricked. Someone had been sending Rarity emails using Pinkie's name. But it was all a lie.

Twilight wasn't sure what texts and emails were, but it certainly seemed like Sunset Shimmer had been causing trouble at Canterlot High for a very long time. All that was about to change, though. And there was just one girl left who needed to know the truth about her friends.

CHAPTER 10

The Definition of a Winner

Rainbow Dash was the only athlete out on the lush, green Canterlot High playing field. There was no game in progress or anything: she was just in the middle of an intense solo practice. Rainbow moved effortlessly, kicking the black-and-white patterned balls into the goal from across the field, one by one. Every single shot she made landed perfectly in the net. It was not that different from the way Twilight had seen Rainbow Dash the Pegasus knock out clouds in the sky over Ponyville. *Boom! Zing! Pow!*

When she kicked the last ball into the net, Applejack ran across the grass to greet her. The rest of the girls watched anxiously from the sidelines. Rainbow Dash looked annoyed at the intrusion.

Rarity tried to remain positive. "They're actually talking. That's a good sign."

From afar, it appeared that Applejack was using a lot of hand gestures, and Rainbow was just standing with her arms crossed. But finally, Applejack and Rainbow Dash hugged.

"Hugs! Hugs are always good," Pinkie chirped, smiling. She clapped her hands together.

Applejack was shaking her head and

smiling as she walked up to the group. "*Somebody* – and I think we can all guess who – told Rainbow Dash my bake sale had been moved to a different day! Dash showed up with the netball team and thought I was the one who'd cancelled on her."

Just as Twilight had suspected! Sunset Shimmer was behind everything.

Rainbow Dash came up to them, kicking a football and laughing. "Yeah! A. J. started to give me the silent treatment. So I started giving *her* the silent treatment. Wasn't about to lose that battle of wills!" Rainbow pointed at Twilight. "Don't know if you've heard, but I don't lose."

Applejack rolled her eyes in a jokey way. Anyone could see that she was relieved to have her best friend Rainbow Dash back. It made Twilight feel warm and fuzzy inside to have helped.

"Now," Rainbow said to Twilight, "all you've got to do to get me to help you out with the whole princess vote is to beat me in a game of one-on-one." She looked smug.

"What?" Twilight's face fell, and her warm feelings turned to nerves. She'd never played football before. Walking on two legs was hard enough! Playing a game on them was going to be no piece of apple tart. But she really needed the athletes to vote for her!

"OK…" Twilight nodded finally.

"First to five goals wins!" Rainbow smiled. Then she took off down the field.

The next twenty minutes were a blur. Everywhere Twilight went, Rainbow Dash was always four steps ahead of her, either blocking her way or stealing the ball. A few times, it seemed like Twilight had a clear shot – and she ended up missing the ball completely and looking really silly. By Rainbow's fourth goal, Twilight knew she was doomed. But she didn't give up.

"Go, Twilight!" Pinkie squealed from the sidelines. "You can do it!"

Twilight surged forward, lifted her leg behind her, and kicked hard. Then…she fell flat on her backside.

"OK, maybe not!" shouted Pinkie with the same enthusiasm. "But good job anyway!"

A moment later, Rainbow kicked goal number five into the net with a satisfied grunt. "That's game!"

It took Twilight a couple of minutes before she was able to catch her breath and stumble back over to the other girls. Rarity gave her a sympathetic look.

"I thought you were really going to pull it out there at the end."

"Yeah, right." Applejack giggled.

"So, what's the plan?" An excited smile spread across Rainbow's face as she jogged up to join them. "How can we make you princess over Sunset Shimmer?"

"But I lost," Twilight said, confused. Rainbow Dash had said that she'd help only if Twilight won the game.

"Of course you lost. I'm awesome." Rainbow smirked, hands on hips. "But I'm not gonna help just anybody. The Fall Formal princess should be someone with heart and determination. And you, Twilight, just proved you've got 'em both!"

The Sweet Shoppe of this realm was quite different from the one back in Ponyville. There were large, cosy sofas everywhere, and the customers sat sipping drinks and reading books. The menu offered cupcakes and slices of pie, and of course, muffins, but there were all sorts of treats listed on the menu that Twilight had never seen before. Mocha Chocolate Bomb? Triple Chocolate Mint Swirl Hot Chocolate? They sounded like Pinkie Pie creations.

Twilight bit her lip as she stared at the big board behind the register. "A Whipped Caramel Strawberry Swirl Shake?" she said to the woman behind the counter, who was busy tittering around, wiping every surface with a pink rag. She looked an awful lot like Mrs Cake with her yellow apron and sweet expression. "And can I get that with extra oats?"

Mrs Cake put down a jug of milk on the counter and gave Twilight a sideways look. "Oats? In a Whipped Caramel Strawberry Swirl Shake?"

Twilight looked over to her friends for guidance. They didn't notice because they were sprawled out on some comfy sofas by the window. They all looked totally wrapped up in the fun atmosphere, just sipping their drinks and chatting. Rarity was scratching under Spike's chin absentmindedly. He looked like he was in heaven, staring up at her with puppy-love eyes. *Typical.* Seeing them sitting there, she smiled. She could almost picture herself staying here – she was getting used to how everyone looked in this realm. She didn't understand why Sunset Shimmer hadn't been able to make the best of it here. She shook her head.

"However you normally make it is fine," Twilight covered, turning back to the counter. Mrs Cake carefully passed her the frothy drink, and Twilight kept her eyes on it as she turned around slowly to join her friends. *BAM!* Milkshake splattered all over the pink-and-yellow tiled floor as Twilight collided with somebody. But a glance up told her that it wasn't just any boy – it was *him*! The cute guy with the spiky blue hair stood there, looking just as flustered as she felt. He started to throw napkins down on the mess.

"We have got to stop bumping into each other like this," he said with a smile, stomping on the soggy napkins with his black-and-white trainers.

"You know me." Twilight laughed

nervously. "I'm always trying to make a big 'splash' around here!" As soon as the words escaped her lips, she regretted them. She sounded like such a dork! Blue-haired boy stared back and raised an eyebrow. "Because my drink kind of splashed on the ground..." Twilight added, wincing. She should probably stop talking now.

The boy chuckled at her and adjusted his black leather jacket.

Great, so now he thought she was totally awkward. Twilight pointed to the sofas stiffly. "I'm going to go over there now." She scampered over to her friends and plopped down on the soft seat. Why was it so difficult to act like a normal pony – *girl* – around him? Twilight took a sip of what was left of her sugary drink and glanced back over her shoulder. He was leaning down, cleaning up the rest of his spilled hot chocolate while Mrs Cake made him another.

Rarity took notice of Twilight's fascination and began to shake her head violently. "Don't even think about it!" Her purple waves swished back and forth. "You're already trying to get her crown. Who knows what Sunset Shimmer would do if you ended up getting her ex-boyfriend, too?"

"I don't even know…we just accidentally…" Twilight said, desperate to deny the implications. Her face grew hot. She hadn't even realised that anyone was watching or who the boy even was. "Ex-boyfriend?"

Fluttershy took a sip of her mint hot chocolate. "Flash Sentry broke up with her a few weeks ago," she explained. The girls' eyes all followed Flash Sentry as he gave Twilight a little wave on his way out of the Sweet Shoppe. Rarity sighed. Clearly, Twilight wasn't the only one around here who thought he was cute.

Fluttershy shook her head. "I can't believe she hasn't done something awful to him yet."

If that were the case, Twilight couldn't help but wonder if Sunset Shimmer was waiting until she had the power to do something *really* awful to him. Power she would get from a certain stolen Equestrian relic. Either way, Twilight thought it was best to keep her distance from Flash Sentry. At least until she got her crown back.

Then it might be negotiable.

CHAPTER 11

The Tails of Twilight Sparkle

Rarity was digging through a giant box of discarded clothes in the back of the Carousel Boutique. It was only down the block from the Sweet Shoppe, and she'd insisted she had to show them all something. It had to do with her brilliant plan to help Twilight get voted as princess, but she wasn't revealing anything yet.

Applejack stood with her arms crossed, an eyebrow raised. "You sure this is going to get folks to see Twilight differently? Differently from the video Sunset Shimmer put online?" She tapped her cowboy boot on the linoleum floor impatiently. This was no time for a fashion show. The dance was tomorrow night!

"Aha!" Rarity exclaimed. She yanked a pair of blue-and-gold plastic triangles connected by a string out of the box. Next, she pulled out a blue-and-gold wig. Apparently, Rarity was oddly obsessed with wigs in this realm. She fastened the triangles on her head and attached the wig to the back of her skirt, admiring herself in the mirror of the nearby dressing room. "I thought we could wear these as a sign of unity."

"OMG!" Fluttershy brightened. "The pony ears and tails we used to wear to show school spirit!"

Applejack, Rainbow Dash and Pinkie Pie dug through the box and found their own sets of matching ears and tails. Applejack did a twirl. "Whoo-eee! These sure were mighty popular freshman year."

"Goooo, Wondercolts!" Pinkie Pie yelled as she leaped across the room in full pink pony wear. She even had some glittery pom-poms and a flag that said CHS on it, though no one saw where she got them from. "I forgot how so totally fun these were! Do I look like a Wondercolt? Do I?! Do I?! Do I?!"

Rarity turned back to the group hopefully. "The five of us are obviously very different, but deep down we're all Canterlot Wondercolts. Sunset Shimmer is the one who divided us. Twilight Sparkle is the one who united us. And we're going to let everybody know it!"

Rarity handed Twilight a blue-and-gold pony tail. "So…what do you think?"

Twilight smiled at her new friends. They all looked so much like her pony friends now. They were almost like… Equestria *girls*. "I think it's a great plan!"

The next day at lunch, the girls were ready to take the Canterlot students by storm. Armed with tons of extra ears and tails, they stepped into the busy cafeteria and got straight to business. The Equestria Girls nodded to one another.

Applejack skipped up to a pair of eco kids. "Vote Twilight Sparkle, y'all!" She handed them some ears and tails. "She's here to unite us, not divide us."

The girls hesitantly took them and put

them on. As soon as they did, they couldn't help but giggle at each other.

Across the room, Fluttershy passed three sets to Apple Bloom, Scootaloo and Sweetie Belle. Since they were freshmen, they'd never worn any before.

"What are these?" Scootaloo chirped with glee.

"My sister used to wear 'em back when she was our age – they rock!" added Apple Bloom. She pointed at Rarity, who was passing some to a pair of fashionistas. "And, look, your sister's wearin' 'em, too, Sweetie Belle!"

Sweetie Belle grabbed a set. "Go, Twilight Sparkle!"

Over at the athletes' table, the football team was taking a little extra convincing. Rainbow Dash walked back and forth like a drill sergeant, sizing them up. "Come on, guys! Twilight's the one who has the real school spirit!" She tossed each of the burly players their own set of ears and tail. As soon as the quarterback, Chance-A-Lot, put his on, the rest of the boys followed suit. "Looking good!"

Even though she still didn't know many of the students, Twilight walked around handing out the Wondercolts pony wear. At every turn, she was greeted with warm smiles and welcoming pats on the back. It seemed like everyone was getting a little excited for someone to finally stand up to Sunset Shimmer. Or they were just curious about the brave new girl.

"Vote for me – *Twilight*," she said, approaching a few interested drama kids. Suddenly, Twilight felt a tap on her shoulder. "Oh! Hi, Flash!" she said, trying to sound casual. He was wearing a set of white ears and a blue tail to match his real hair. It looked a little silly stuck to his jeans, but in a good way. Now that she looked at him more closely, he sort of reminded her of somepony...

Sunset Shimmer burst through the doors in a rage.

"Looks great!" Twilight replied, and dashed away before Sunset could see her talking to him.

"This is ridiculous!" Sunset Shimmer flipped her fiery hair and took in the scene. Everybody in the whole cafeteria was now wearing ears and tails – and they were all *enjoying* themselves. And the name on their lips? *Twilight Sparkle.*

But if Sunset Shimmer had anything to say about it, Twilight's party would soon be over and Sunset's coronation would begin . . .

CHAPTER 12

A Frame and a Flash

"Doesn't everyone look fabulous?" Rarity beamed as her fellow Equestria Girls – Rainbow Dash, Fluttershy, Pinkie Pie, Applejack and Twilight Sparkle – strutted down the hallway in their new accessories. Everyone they passed was also wearing the ears and tails. It was just like freshman year again!

"It was a great idea, Rarity," agreed Twilight.

Sunset Shimmer came up behind them, smiling. She made a point to bump into Applejack as she passed by.

Applejack frowned. "Don't know what she's smiling about. Twilight's the one who's going to be princess of the Fall Formal."

"Yeah, she is!" Rainbow cheered as she high-fived Applejack.

"Is she going to Principal Celestia's office?" Fluttershy observed. "Oh no."

Sunset Shimmer knocked on the office door, a wicked look in her eye. She was definitely up to no good. The door opened and Vice Principal Luna was there. She looked down at Sunset, concerned.

Sunset frowned dramatically. "Vice Principal Luna, something terrible has happened! The dance is ruined!" She threw her hand up to her forehead like she was about to faint from the shock of it all. Rainbow Dash scoffed.

"What do you mean, Sunset Shimmer?" Vice Principal Luna asked. It was obvious that she didn't entirely trust the girl, either.

"You don't believe me? Come and see for yourself!" She shot Twilight a triumphant look. "All the decorations are totally ruined."

Pinkie Pie's face fell. "What?!" Pinkie had been working on the decorations for days and days. Sunset had to be bluffing. There was no way she was *that* evil.

Vice Principal Luna sighed and motioned for Sunset to lead the way to the gym. The girls all followed.

It was evident from the front entrance of the gym that something was wrong. The banner that used to read CANTERLOT

FALL FORMAL had been torn down and lay on the floor in tatters. Pinkie gasped in horror. But the worst was yet to come. A smirk danced on the corners of Sunset Shimmer's mouth as she pushed open the gym doors.

Inside, everything looked terrible. The balloons had all been popped and the streamers ripped down. The tables were overturned and all the cases of fizzy drink had been smashed across the floor. Pinkie whimpered in despair. She tried to pinch her own arm to make sure she wasn't dreaming. It couldn't be true!

"Isn't this just awful? And after Pinkie Pie worked so *hard* to make things perfect." Sunset Shimmer batted her eyelashes innocently. "Why would Twilight Sparkle do something like this?"

Twilight's stomach churned. Of course

this was Sunset's plan – to pin a crime on her so she couldn't run for princess. It was really sneaky.

"Twilight Sparkle? Why would you think Twilight was responsible for something like this?" Vice Principal Luna looked to Twilight, unconvinced.

"Because I have proof," Sunset snapped. She stepped forward and handed a stack of papers to Vice Principal Luna, who inspected them. Luna took a deep breath and turned to Twilight. She looked concerned. "I think you both had better come to my office."

Five minutes later, Twilight and Sunset sat across from Vice Principal Luna. A series of photographs was spread across the desk. Sunset wore a smug expression, but every time Luna looked up, Sunset would make a big show of frowning. It was so transparent.

"This is clearly you in the photographs, is it not?" Vice Principal Luna said, passing Twilight a photo. She couldn't believe what she saw. The photo had been made to look like Twilight was kicking over a table in the gym. Bottles of fizzy drink were flying through the air, and everything around her was trashed. But how?

"Yes, it's me, but – I didn't do this!" Twilight exclaimed.

"Photographs don't lie, Twilight," Luna said. "But as the chief disciplinarian at this school, I have learned that students do. Especially when they get caught red-handed." Luna shook her head, disappointed. "I think it should be fairly obvious that the school cannot let someone who would do something like this compete for the Fall Formal crown."

Twilight slumped down in her chair.

She was starting to think she'd under-estimated her rival. This was exactly what Sunset Shimmer wanted. It was the second time in the span of two days that she'd undercut Twilight's campaign for princess. What was a girl to do now? She had to get the crown and leave through the portal *tonight*.

Suddenly, the door burst open. It was Flash Sentry!

"Vice Principal Luna, I found these in a rubbish bin in the library. Thought you should see them." He shot Sunset Shimmer a dirty look and handed a set of photos over to Luna. The expression on her face changed instantly.

"What are they?" snarled Sunset. She craned her neck to get a look.

"They are proof that someone was

trying to frame Twilight Sparkle," said Luna. She held up a photo of Twilight kicking a football. It was identical to the one of her kicking over the table. "Someone must have combined these photos of her playing football with pictures of the gym."

Sunset feigned shock. "Oh, really? That's terrible!"

Vice Principal Luna stood. "I appreciate you bringing this to my attention, Flash." She nodded at Twilight. "In light of this new evidence, you may of course continue your bid to be crowned the princess of the Fall Formal."

"But she—!" Sunset whined.

"Thank you! You have no idea how important this is to me." Twilight jumped up and threw her arms around Flash. He stumbled backwards, laughing. Sunset

Shimmer flipped her hair and stormed out of the office.

Flash Sentry shrugged. "I wouldn't be much of a Canterlot Wondercolt if I didn't try to prove your innocence, would I?"

Twilight let go of him, flustered. What had gotten into her? She told herself it was just the excitement of him rescuing her. Yes – that was it.

"I have to go get ready for the dance!" Twilight announced, smiling. She made her way to the door. She realised she didn't have anything to wear and—

"Oh, actually…I'm afraid so much damage has been done to the gym that we will have to postpone the dance until tomorrow night," Luna said, interrupting Twilight's excited thoughts. She opened the office door. "If you'll excuse me—"

"So, uh, Twilight, I was wondering…"

Flash looked down at the floor. "If you aren't already going with somebody, do you want to go to the Fall Formal with me tomorrow night?"

Twilight suddenly felt very nervous. "That would be—" Wait – *what?!* Flash had just asked her to the dance…but for *tomorrow* night. By then, the portal would be closed! By then, she would be stuck here in this realm for thirty moons. By then, everypony back in Equestria would be in danger without the Elements of Harmony to protect them!

"No, no, no!" Twilight shook her head and dashed to the door, leaving Flash Sentry standing alone. "That'll be too late!" Twilight shouted as she ran out into the hall.

It was bad enough that the dance was rescheduled, but to add insult to injury,

Twilight had just completely ditched Flash. He had no idea what he'd done to offend her so badly.

One *no* would have been enough.

CHAPTER 13

The Truth About Equestria

Twilight wasn't sure why she was standing in the Carousel Boutique wearing a completely ridiculous blue frock that Rarity had chosen. She didn't feel much like trying on dresses right now. Not since everything was a mess. She still had no crown, and the portal was closing tonight.

A soft knock sounded on her dressing room door. "Everything OK in there?" Rarity sing-songed.

"Yes," Twilight lied. Spike looked up at her, trying to communicate through his puppy-dog eyes so he wouldn't give himself away by talking. He looked just as worried as she was.

"If I don't get my crown tonight, I won't be able to go back for another thirty moons!" she whispered. "What are we going to do?"

Spike looked around to make sure it was safe to talk. "We tell them the truth. They'll help us figure something out!"

"But what if they won't?" Twilight bit her lip like she'd seen the girl version of Rarity do a few times. She was getting better at copying the mannerisms of these creatures. "What if they find out just how different I really am...?"

"Twilight, these girls rallied around you because they saw what was in your heart." Spike jumped up on the dressing-room stool. "They aren't going to feel any different about you when they find out you're a pony princess in Equestria."

As she faced herself in the mirror, Twilight realised that Spike was completely right. These girls had become her friends. Telling them the truth was worth a shot – it might be the only way she would see her other friends ever again!

Twilight leaned down and patted Spike on the head. She was glad he'd managed to sneak through the portal behind her after all. He seemed to be glad, too. If they got stuck for another thirty moons, however, that might change.

"Here goes nothing, Spike," Twilight said as she pushed open her dressing-room door.

"You OK, Twilight Sparkle?" Applejack

instantly noticed the look on Twilight's face. Like she was keeping something in.

"Well, the Fall Formal isn't happening tonight because of Sunset Shimmer, right?" Twilight paced around her friends, working up the courage to explain.

"Well, yeah, but it's still going to be awesome when it happens tomorrow night!" Rainbow Dash said. She was riffling through a rack of sequined dresses and having no luck choosing one.

This was going to be hard. Twilight took a deep breath. "I'm sure it would be – but the Fall Formal *has* to happen tonight. You see—"

Pinkie Pie held a satiny fuchsia frock up to her body and looked at herself in the mirror. She turned to Twilight, wide-eyed. "Because you're from an alternate world and you're a pony princess there and the crown actually has a magical element embedded in it that helps power up other magical elements and without it they don't work any more and you need them to help protect your magical world and if you don't get the crown tonight you'll be stuck in this world and won't be able to get back for like a really long time?"

Twilight's jaw dropped. The rest of the girls looked at Pinkie as though she'd gone insane.

"Yeah, I'm pretty sure that isn't the reason," Rainbow said, rolling her eyes.

Spike stood up on two legs. "No, she's pretty much spot-on," he said.

Rarity gasped at Spike. "He can talk?!" She looked around in horror, as if the dresses might stand up and walk out of the room, too.

Spike winked at her. "Oh yeah. And

back where I come from, I'm not even a dog. I am a ferocious fire-breathing dragon!"

"Oh my gosh!" Fluttershy skipped over. She knelt down and began to inspect him like a science experiment. "This is soooo amazing. Tell me, what are you thinking right now?"

Twilight didn't notice any of it. She just stood there, completely shocked at Pinkie Pie's accurate guess. "How did you know all that?"

Pinkie smiled and shrugged. "Just a hunch!"

"Wait a minute." Applejack walked over to Twilight. The novelty of a talking dog had worn off for a second. "Let me get this straight. You're a pony?"

"You're a princess?" Rarity asked, totally in awe.

"You're from another world?" said Fluttershy, mouth agape.

Twilight could easily solve this right now by telling them it had all been a joke. Then they wouldn't be looking at her like that. Like she had two heads. But Spike had already spoken and then she wouldn't have *any* chance of getting the crown.

"Yes, I am," Twilight announced, ready for the backlash.

"That…" said Rainbow Dash, breaking into a smile, "is…awesome!"

It turned out Spike was right after all. Her new friends didn't care what she was – girl, girl wearing pony ears, or actual pony. They just liked *her*. And that was even more awesome.

CHAPTER 14

A Chance for the Dance

There wasn't much time to fix it, but the girls had all gathered at the gym to assess the damage caused by Sunset Shimmer, Snips and Snails. Maybe, if they all worked together, they would be able to get the dance back up and running for tonight. Twilight hoped so, at least. The gym looked pretty awful.

Rarity picked through a pile of ripped party streamers. "I simply can't believe they did all this."

Pinkie had been upset at first, but now she was bouncing around with excitement. She saw the situation as an opportunity to have fun decorating all over again. And this time it would be with her friends! "Now, if only I had some sort of party cannon that could decorate everything super fast..." She plucked the remains of a balloon arch off the shiny floor and threw it into a rubbish bag. "I think we can fix this up by tonight, no problem!"

"Let's do it, y'all!" cheered Applejack, extending her hand.

"Absolutely," Rarity joined in.

"Rock on!" shouted Rainbow as she placed her hand on top of Rarity's.

"Yes-indeedily!" chirped Pinkie.

"Yaaaaay," Fluttershy attempted to yell, but it came out very soft.

Twilight grinned and put her hand on top. "Go, Equestria Girls!"

"Woo-hoo!" shouted a few random voices. The girls turned around to see a big group of students, all wearing Wondercolts gear. They stood waiting at the double doors carrying bags of new decorations, bunches of balloons and multiple ladders. But the most amazing part was that they were kids from every group at school – the athletes, the fashionistas, the techies, the dramas and the eco kids!

"We came to see if you guys wanted any help," said Chance-A-Lot, adjusting his pony ears. Everybody behind him nodded along. "If we're going to have the dance tonight, we thought you might need it!" A few shouts and cries escaped from the group.

Twilight smiled. "That'd be great!" She couldn't believe it!

"Yippeeeee!" shouted Pinkie Pie. It had been ages since she'd had so many helpers. Everyone spread out across the gym and got to work cleaning up the mess. It looked like the students of Canterlot High were finally ready to band together again – to help one another out and make friends with kids from other groups. Seeing everyone together almost made Twilight happier than the prospect of getting her crown back. *Almost.*

It was incredible what everyone could accomplish when they worked together. In just a few short hours, the gym went from an ultimate disaster to a gorgeous magical land. Pinkie had done a fantastic job directing the efforts, and now it looked even better than it had the first time!

Curly ribbons of blue, pink and purple hung from the ceiling. Streamers were draped from every corner of the gym towards the centre, creating an effect that made it seem more like a grand ballroom than a basketball court. And, of course, shiny balloons were tied to the back of every chair and to every table. Principal Celestia declared the Fall Formal was back on for that night!

"I still can't believe we pulled it off," said Fluttershy. She did a little twirl to try out the dance floor.

"I can." Rainbow Dash looked satisfied. She shrugged. "We're awesome."

"Enough chatter, girls!" Rarity said, looking at the clock on the wall. "We need to get ready. And we need to look fabulous!"

Right now, everyone was looking a little bit tired from all the heavy labour. But if there was one thing Rarity was talented at – it was making her friends look amazing. A trip to the Carousal Boutique was just the thing they all needed. Twilight had to look like a princess, after all.

CHAPTER 15

The Canterlot High School Coronation

Twilight beamed as she climbed out of the stretch limo. It was finally time for the Fall Formal – time to win back her crown. She was extremely proud of how her friends had all come together to make sure the dance still happened. Plus, Rarity had chosen excellent gowns that highlighted each of the girls' best features. It almost felt like the night she went to the Grand Galloping Gala in Canterlot. Only this time, Twilight was wearing a stunning, sparkly pink dress and walking on two legs instead.

"I feel only *slightly* less tough in this dress," joked Rainbow Dash as she climbed out of the limo. The look *was* less sporty than she was used to, but she looked really pretty. The dress matched her hair perfectly. The snug bodice had a stripe of each rainbow colour, and a ruffled red skirt flared out from the bottom.

Fluttershy, Pinkie Pie and Applejack all followed next. Each of their dresses reflected their personalities perfectly – right down to Pinkie's over-the-top poufy party frock with a giant bow around the waist. "PARTYYYY!" Pinkie squealed, jumping up and down with glee.

"Hurry on up, Rarity!" Applejack said, smoothing down her blue denim frock. It had a row of red apples along the hem. It was understated and a little more casual – just like the girl wearing it. "We need to get on inside so Twilight can get her crown!"

"I'm coming, *darlings*. I just had to touch up my lipgloss!" Rarity stepped out of the limo with a flourish. Her short blue party dress was all ruffles and sequins. She wore tall white boots adorned with shimmery jewels. "Now, how do I look?"

"You look beautiful, Rarity," Twilight said. She helped Spike out of the limo. He was even wearing a little doggy tuxedo for the occasion. He kept trying to get Rarity to notice, but she was too busy looking at her hair in the reflection of the car window.

The girls linked arms and walked across the front lawn towards the school, passing right by the Wondercolt statue. Twilight noticed that the moon was directly over it, shining down on the portal. It was almost perfectly in line. She suspected that by the time tonight was over, it wouldn't be any more.

"Twilight!" Flash Sentry called out as he hopped out of a red sports car. Rarity and Applejack raised their eyebrows at each other. He looked mighty excited to see Twilight. Even though she'd denied any sort of crush, they were starting to wonder.

He jogged up to meet them. "Twilight…I know you said no about going to the Fall Formal with me but… uh…maybe you'd reconsider and at least have one dance?"

"I didn't say no!" Twilight replied. "I mean, I did, but I didn't mean 'no' to *you*…I was…what I mean is…" She wasn't making any sense! Finally, she blurted out, "Yes, I'd love to dance with you."

Flash grinned. The girls all giggled and began to whisper to one another.

"Let's go inside," said Twilight Sparkle, blushing.

Inside the Canterlot gym, the dance was already in full swing. The disco ball spun around, creating a million tiny lights across every balloon, streamer and smiling student.

It really is magical here, thought Twilight as she entered the room.

Up on the stage, the DJ was spinning a remix of an old favourite, "Raise This

Barn". She had blue hair and wore reflective sunglasses even though it was dark in the room, but it looked super cool. And over in the corner, Granny Smith was serving cups of fresh fizzy apple juice.

"Eeeeee! Come on!" Pinkie shrieked, skipping over to the dance floor. She jumped so much that her tiny blue top hat almost fell off. "I can't wait to get my groovy-woovy groove on!"

The Equestria Girls laughed and followed Pinkie out onto the dance floor to do the same.

When the DJ's set was over, Flash Sentry and his band took to the stage. They fired up the room, starting to play a cover of a pop song that the whole gym knew the words to. Everyone who had been standing around on the sides of the gym rushed onto the dance floor.

"Thanks, Canterlot High!" Flash Sentry said into the microphone. "We're Flash Drive! Come see us play at the Sweet Shoppe next weekend." Then he winked at Twilight from the stage, and they broke out into another upbeat song. Twilight hoped no one had seen, especially her rival. The last thing she needed right now was a fight over a boy!

Twilight scanned the crowded room. "Anybody seen Sunset Shimmer?"

"Maybe she's too embarrassed to show," Rainbow shouted as she pumped her fist in the air to the music. "She's gotta know you won by a landslide!"

"Yeah, maybe." Twilight bit her lip. She wished she could feel as confident about winning as Rainbow always seemed to be. Because this time – winning really would matter.

The students all watched with bated breath as Principal Celestia walked up onto the stage. It was finally time to announce the princess of the Fall Formal! So much was riding on the next few moments. Twilight felt her hands start to dampen, which was a new sensation. It must have been nerves.

Principal Celestia smiled at the sea of dressed-up students. She looked beautiful this evening as well – she wore an elegant purple dress that complemented her pastel hair. Vice Principal Luna had opted for a midnight-blue gown that accented her darker features. She stood nearby, holding a wooden box. The crown was definitely in there. *So close*, thought Twilight.

"First of all, I want to say how wonderful everything looks tonight. You all did a magnificent job pulling things together after the unfortunate events of earlier today."

A few mumbles broke through the crowd. Not everyone at school knew that Twilight had been accused of trashing the gym, but rumours about the incident and people trying to guess who had done such a thing had been flying around all afternoon.

Celestia cleared her throat. "And now, without further ado, I'd like to announce the winner of this year's Fall Formal crown."

Fluttershy patted Twilight on the back reassuringly. Pinkie Pie bounced up and down in anticipation. Twilight just tried to keep breathing.

"The princess of this year's Fall Formal is..." Principal Celestia tore open the golden envelope with a flourish. "Twilight Sparkle!"

The gym erupted in cheers. *We did it!*

"Omigosh, I was so nervous," Fluttershy squeaked.

Pinkie Pie blew into a noisemaker. "Wahoooooooo!"

Celestia motioned to Twilight, and she walked up the steps carefully. This would be the worst time to fall, even if it was called the *Fall* Formal. She reminded herself to smile, too. Everyone seemed so happy for her. Down below, her friends were all clapping. Twilight didn't see Sunset Shimmer, but that didn't mean she wasn't still sulking in some dark corner of the gym right now.

"Congratulations, Twilight!" whispered Principal Celestia as she took the crown from the wooden box and placed it atop

Twilight's head. The second it touched her hair, Twilight felt an instant wave of relief wash over her. Everypony was going to be safe now. She would go back through the portal tonight and home to Equestria as planned. Harmony would be restored.

But the good feelings didn't last for long.

"Twilight! Help!" a familiar voice rang out through the gym.

"Spike?" Twilight said, scanning the crowd for him. "Is that you?" It wouldn't make much sense for him to be speaking right now. In this world, dogs weren't supposed to talk, and in a big crowd like this, everyone would hear him! So why was he causing a commotion? This wasn't the best time.

Then Twilight saw. Snips was cackling as he ran out of the gym, holding Spike under his arm. Suddenly, the world melted away. "They've got Spike!" she called out to her friends. Twilight jumped down from the stage and ran after them, parting the crowds of confused students.

"Spike!" she called out. Spike squirmed and reached out for Twilight, but Snails followed close behind his partner and blocked her. Twilight rushed out the door after them. Pinkie Pie, Applejack, Fluttershy, Rainbow Dash and Rarity were all on her heels.

Once they were all outside, Twilight spotted Snips and Snails tearing across the Canterlot High front lawn. "There!" she shouted. They were going straight for the statue of the Wondercolt. Straight towards the portal!

"That's close enough," Sunset Shimmer said, stepping out from behind the statue.

"Don't hurt him," Twilight pleaded. Spike looked really scared. Now she understood the meaning of the phrase *puppy-dog eyes.*

"Oh, I wouldn't dream of it." Sunset began to pace back and forth. "I'm not a monster, Twilight." She whipped around and barked at Snips, "Let him go."

"What do you want?" asked Twilight.

"I just wanted your attention so I could say congrats on your big win." From the tone of Sunset's voice, Twilight didn't think she meant it in the slightest. "Too bad you won't be able to take your crown home with you."

Sunset Shimmer turned on her heel and bent down to pick something up. It was a long silver stick with a knob on the end of it.

"A golf club? Oooooh, is this a secret

night golf party?!" Pinkie Pie couldn't help herself. "Or is it like a golf club *club*? I don't like the game much, but I suppose I could join…"

Sunset Shimmer shot Pinkie a look, and the girl clammed up. This was no time to annoy Sunset.

Sunset held the stick high above her – right above the portal and perfectly poised to destroy it. Sunset smiled deviously. "Say goodbye to Equestria, Princess," she cackled.

This couldn't be happening. *No, no, no!* A moment ago, back at the dance, everything had been perfect. Twilight had been voted Fall Formal princess, received her crown, and was all set to return home to Equestria tonight, just in the nick of time. Now Sunset Shimmer was threatening to destroy the only way she could get back home…*for ever*. Twilight had to do something.

"You don't belong here. Give me back the crown and you can go back to Equestria tonight." Sunset Shimmer tapped the base of the statue with the golf club. "Or keep it and never go home."

Twilight didn't know what to do. Neither option was going to work. If she handed the crown over, the Elements of Harmony would be rendered useless. They needed one another to work. But if she kept the crown, Twilight could never return home. Which would also be useless. And then she'd never see her Ponyville friends again!

"Tick-tock, Twilight. We haven't got all night. The portal will be closing on its own in less than an hour," said Sunset. She looked at her wrist, even though she wasn't wearing a watch. "So…what's your answer?"

Something snapped inside of Twilight, and she stamped her foot. This was ridiculous. Sunset Shimmer couldn't get away with destroying everything that mattered just because she was upset about being unpopular.

Twilight narrowed her eyes. "No."

"What?!" Sunset squawked, her eyes fiery. "Don't you see what I'm about to do to the portal?"

Twilight stood tall. She knew that her Canterlot High friends were right there with her … She might not be at home with all the Elements of Harmony, but she still had the most important thing – friendship. "Yes, but I've also seen what you've been able to do here without magic. Equestria will find a way to survive without my

Element of Harmony. This place might not if I allow it to fall into your hands." Twilight took a few steps closer to Sunset. "So go ahead. Destroy the portal. You *aren't* getting this crown."

"Fine." Sunset Shimmer dropped the golf club to the ground, defeated. "You win. Come on, Snips! Snails!" she snapped, and the pair fell in line. Twilight breathed a sigh of relief. The portal was safe, and she still had her crown.

"Can't believe you were going to do that for us!" said Applejack.

"It's no wonder you're a real live princess," added Rarity.

"Yes, she's so very *special.*" Sunset Shimmer leaned in close to Twilight's face. "Take your crown back to Equestria, Princess Twilight. See if I care."

And in one swift motion, Sunset

Shimmer reached for the crown. Fortunately, Twilight's reflexes as a two-legged creature were getting better. She dived out of Sunset's grasp and went tumbling onto the grass. The crown flew off Twilight's head and landed about two feet away, jewel-side down.

Sunset lunged for it, but Spike was quicker. He snatched the crown and took off across the lawn, carrying it in his little dog mouth.

"Grab him, you fools!" Sunset Shimmer yelled at Snips and Snails. "He's headed for the gym!"

The two boys raced after him, tripping several times. Twilight and her friends followed, though it wasn't easy to move fast in their high heels and dresses. Rainbow Dash shot forward. She didn't let anything hold her back.

"Over here, Spike!" shouted Rainbow from inside the front doors of the gym. He darted through the legs of the students and attempted to fling the crown in her direction. Rainbow caught it perfectly and jumped up onto a large speaker. Snips was right below!

Rainbow Dash hooked her arm through the crown and reached for the nearby basketball hoop. She swung on the metal ring and flung her body onto the stage like an acrobat. The satisfied smirk on her face vanished as soon as Snails popped up beside her.

"Heads up!" she shouted as she threw the crown to Spike again. He jumped high and caught it in his mouth. Before he could run back to Twilight, he was lifted into the air.

"I'll take that," Sunset Shimmer said,

grabbing him around the belly and stealing the crown straight out of his mouth. She dropped him on the ground and closed her eyes, relishing her final victory. "At last! More power than I could ever imagine!" She marvelled at the crown glinting under the light of the disco ball.

Confused students stopped dancing and started to back away from the crazed Sunset, creating a circle around her. Her eyes turned fiery as she stared at her precious prize.

PHZAAAM! A bright flash suddenly flooded the gym with red light, temporarily blinding the crowd.

When everyone's vision returned, something that was neither girl nor pony stood before them. And it was terrifying.

CHAPTER 16

The True Colours of Sunset

The frightening creature paced around the circle, laughing at the crowd of scared students. Her hair and tail seemed like they were made of fire, with flames licking up around her and the gnarled horn on her head. Her massive dragon-like wings extended out behind her, and her skin was tinted red. As she looked around the gym, an expression of contempt flashed across her green eyes.

The creature threw her head back and cackled wickedly.

She raised her clawed hands and shot two fireballs out. They hit Snips and Snails – instantly transforming them into hybrid creatures as well. They each sprouted wings, giving them a sort of an evil boy-Pegasus look.

Chills went down Twilight's spine. Was this Sunset Shimmer's true form? All this time she'd thought Sunset was just some pony from Canterlot, which was clearly not the case. Whatever she was, she was not friendly. But she had Twilight's crown and now she was terrorising the school for real.

There was only one thing left to do.

Twilight lunged for the Sunset creature, but the thing shot two more fireballs in Twilight's direction, both of which she narrowly avoided by ducking. Sunset laughed.

"I have to say, I am really disappointed in all of you. I've had to jump through so many hoops tonight to get my hands on this crown and it really should have been mine all along. But let's let bygones be bygones. I am your princess now. And you will be loyal to *me*."

The girls watched in horror as Sunset approached a group of students who were cowering in the corner of the gym. She shot a few more blasts of fire, and suddenly they were all like zombies. Their bodies looked stiff, and their eyes were glazed red.

Sunset turned to Snips and Snails. "Round them up and bring them to the portal!" Then she turned to Twilight and her friends, a big smile on her face.

"Spoiler alert: I was bluffing back there when I said I was going to destroy the portal. I don't want to rule this pathetic little high school! I want Equestria! And with my own little teenage army behind me, I'm going to get it."

"No." Twilight stood up. "You're not."

"Oh, please. I have magic, and you have *nothing*."

Rainbow Dash was the first to stand up behind Twilight, arms crossed.

"She has us," Applejack joined in, followed by Pinkie Pie, Rarity and Fluttershy.

Sunset Shimmer feigned shock. "OMG! The gang really is all back together again. It's just like freshman year." She walked up to Pinkie Pie, who was doing her best to put on a tough face. "Now step aside. Twilight has tried to interfere with my plans one too many times already. She needs to be dealt with."

If they were anything like her Ponyville friends, Twilight knew that they wouldn't abandon her now. Sure enough, Sunset Shimmer fired a blast of fiery red light at them, but the girls all clasped hands and braced themselves for the worst.

"What is happening?!" yelled Sunset Shimmer as the six girls rose up into the air. They became enveloped in a bright white light. When they landed on the ground again, each girl's hair had grown out into long pony tails and they had real pony ears. Plus, Fluttershy and Rainbow Dash now had wings and Rarity was sporting a Unicorn horn.

The white light then passed through Twilight. She also rose up into the air, spun around, and landed with her own horn and wings. Twilight breathed a sigh of relief. Even though she wasn't completely transformed into her pony self, she already felt better. Well, as good as she could feel for someone in a gym full of zombie-students and a scary fire monster.

"I don't understand!" Sunset Shimmer cried out in despair.

Twilight stepped forward, head held high. She gestured at her friends, who were looking at one another in awe. Rainbow Dash was trying to flap her wings, but the rest stood frozen.

"The magic contained in my Element was able to unite with those that helped save it. The same Elements that exist in Equestria can be found in this world – Honesty, Kindness, Laughter, Generosity and Loyalty. Together with the crown, they create a power beyond anything you could imagine. But it is a power that you don't have the ability to control."

Twilight pointed to the monster. "The crown may be upon your head, Sunset Shimmer, but you cannot wield it, because you do not possess the most powerful magic of all – the Magic of Friendship. It is the only magic that can truly unite us all."

Apparently, they were magic words, because as soon as she'd said them, Twilight and her friends rose up together once more. A powerful blast of rainbow light surged from them, striking Sunset Shimmer. The crown tumbled off her head and onto the ground. And the spell was broken at last.

Chapter 17

After the Sun Sets

It was as if they'd all awoken from a strange dream. Students rubbed their eyes as their senses returned to them. They were unharmed, but confused and groggy nonetheless. Even though the Equestria Girls still had their long hair and pony ears, everyone else was back to normal, including the one who had caused it all.

Sunset Shimmer lay curled up on the

gym floor, transformed back to her former girl self. As she blinked herself awake, Sunset looked around at her fellow students. They stared down at her with disdain. She shrank back and hugged her knees, as vulnerable as ever. Twilight felt sort of bad for her, but that didn't change what she had just done to Canterlot High.

"You will never rule in Equestria," said Twilight, approaching Sunset. "And any power you may have had in this world is gone. Tonight you've shown everyone who you really are. You've shown them all what is in your heart."

"I'm sorry." Sunset Shimmer shook her head and began to cry. "I'm so sorry. I didn't know there was another way!"

"The Magic of Friendship doesn't just exist in Equestria. It's everywhere." Twilight motioned to the vast gym around her, filled with students. Filled with potential friends. "You can seek it out. Or you can be for ever alone. The choice is yours."

Sunset sniffed. "All I've done since I've been here is drive everyone apart. I don't know the first thing about friendship."

Luckily, there were five girls who would be willing to teach her a thing or two. Pinkie Pie, Fluttershy, Applejack, Rainbow Dash and Rarity all approached the sad girl and began to help her up. She looked up at them, wide-eyed. Like she couldn't believe people could ever be kind to someone just because it was nice to be nice. It wasn't much, but it was a start.

Principal Celestia approached Twilight. She had the crown in her hands. "I believe this belongs to you," she said, placing the crown atop Twilight's head once more.

Vice Principal Luna nodded her agreement. "A true princess in any world leads not by forcing others to bow before her, but by inspiring others to stand with her. We have all seen that you are capable of just that. I hope you see it, too, Princess Twilight Sparkle."

"I do," Twilight replied as regally as she could. Once she got back to Equestria, she would need to take some time to really let the events of the past three days sink in and—

"So would now be a completely awkward time to ask you for that dance?" Flash Sentry popped up, completely interrupting Twilight's train of thought. He bit his lip nervously as he waited for her response.

Twilight smiled. She supposed there was time for at least *one* dance.

Chapter 18

Back to Equestria

It was going to be sad to leave them, but Twilight was glad that her new friends were all back together again. They had one another, and that was what mattered! And now they also had an unexpected new friend as well – Sunset Shimmer – who seemed to be already embracing the idea of being nice instead of evil.

"You'll look out for her, won't you?" Twilight said to her friends. They were standing at the front by the statue. Their faces were only lit by moonlight, but Twilight could tell that they were going to miss her, too. Pinkie Pie's bottom lip jutted out and began to quiver.

"Of course we will," answered Rarity. "Though I do expect some sort of apology for last spring's video debacle."

Twilight patted Rarity on the back. "I have a feeling she'll be handing out a lot of apologies."

They'd all been busy dancing, but Twilight had noticed Sunset going around the gym, apologising to several students. Luckily, most of them had no idea what she was talking about because they'd been in a trance during her little fiery tantrum. But it still showed that she wanted to change.

Spike barked and wagged his tail.

"We'd better get going," he said, gesturing to the portal. "We don't want the others to worry."

He was right. Twilight couldn't put it off any longer, or else she risked missing the portal altogether. Being stuck here for thirty more moons no longer felt like it would be the worst thing in the world, but everypony back home needed her.

"I'll miss you girls!" Twilight enveloped her friends in a group hug. Then she reached out to Spike. They stepped up to the statue. The surface of it glimmered and gleamed just as the mirror had back in Equestria. It was now or never...

She turned to Spike. "Ready?"

The purple pony and baby dragon were blinded by white light as they stepped out of the mirror in the Crystal Castle. They couldn't see anything, but they could hear lots of voices.

"Twilight!" shouted Pinkie Pie.

"You're back!" cheered Applejack.

"You got your crown!" Rarity sighed.

"Psht, I knew you could do it," stated Rainbow Dash.

Twilight blinked her eyes and sure enough, there they all were. Her pony friends! They looked like they hadn't left the mirror's side since she'd gone through the portal. But their relieved faces told her everything she needed to know. She was back, and Equestria was safe once more.

"Sunset Shimmer," asked Princess Celestia, anxiously approaching the weary traveller. "Is she all right?"

"I think she's going to be fine. I left her in very good hands," Twilight assured the princess.

Rainbow Dash made a funny face. "What are hands?"

Twilight and Spike smiled at each other. If only they knew the half of it!

"Come on, everypony," Celestia said as she followed Cadance and Luna out of the mirror room. They'd spent the better part of three days in there, waiting anxiously for Twilight. Now that she was back, it was definitely time to go and get some fresh air.

Of course, Twilight's Ponyville friends had a million questions for her about the mysterious other realm. Pinkie Pie bounced around the group in a circle as they walked along.

"I want to tell you everything, I do!" Twilight stopped in her tracks. "But I'm just so exhausted from all the dancing."

"Dancing?" Rarity probed. She trotted forward, eyes sparkling with delight. "Tell me more!"

Twilight began to laugh as she backed away. Then, "Oooof!" Twilight suddenly felt her body smack straight into something solid.

"We've got to stop bumping into each other like this," the blue-haired royal guard pony said. He grinned at Twilight like he was laughing at some private joke. She watched with fascination as he trotted off.

"Who was that?"

"He's a new member of the Crystal Castle Royal Guard," Princess Cadance said. "Why? Do you know him?"

Twilight chuckled. "Not exactly…"

"Somebody's got a crush on the new guy!" Applejack sing-songed. She nudged Twilight playfully.

"No, I don't!"

"She does. She absolutely does." Rarity nodded.

"Don't be ridiculous. I don't even. He just—" Twilight tried to argue, but the ponies trotted along, giggling.

Pinkie took a deep breath like she was about to dive underwater or blow up a giant balloon. "He just totally reminds you of a guy you met in that other world who played guitar and was in a band and helped prove you didn't destroy all the decorations for a big dance so you could still run for princess of the big dance and then asked you to dance at that dance … Right?"

Twilight Sparkle stopped. "How did you know that, Pinkie Pie?"

Pinkie shrugged and skipped ahead. "Just a hunch."

Twilight laughed and shook her head as she ran up to join the other ponies. She was glad that she'd visited the other realm. But there was nothing better than being back home in Equestria with her very own best friends.

Through the Mirror

Princess Celestia taught
Princess Twilight Sparkle, and now
Princess Twilight Sparkle is
going to teach you!
Turn the page for some
magical assignments!

In Their Element

List the names of your best friends
and an Element of Harmony that
really shines within each of them.
Example: Rarity, Generosity

_____

_____

_____

_____

_____

_____

_____

_____

_____

_____

Friends of a Feather

Why do you think you and your
friends get along so well? Write about
how your Elements of Harmony
come together.

_____

_____

_____

_____

_____

_____

_____

_____

_____

_____

Canterlot School Spirit

If you and your friends got a touch of magic and became Equestria Girls, how would you pony-fy yourselves? Draw the details here!

A Shimmer of Hope

Do you know anyone like Sunset Shimmer –
someone who acts mean but probably
just feels lonely and needs a friend?
Write about that person here.

_____

_____

_____

_____

_____

_____

_____

_____

_____

List some ideas of how you could show this person that you are willing to be friends. Example: smile at them in the corridor.

_____

_____

_____

_____

_____

_____

_____

_____

_____

The Meaning of Magic

Write about what friendship means to you!

_____

_____

_____

_____

_____

_____

_____

_____

_____

_____

_____

_____

Princess Summit Agenda

What do you think Celestia and the
other princesses need to discuss?
Come up with an official agenda
for their summit!

Equestria Princess Summit Agenda

Opening remarks from Princess Mi Amore Cadenza

First discussion topic: _____

A presentation on the Elements of Harmony by
Princess Twilight Sparkle

Second discussion topic: _____

A presentation on Canterlot history by Princess
Celestia

Third discussion topic: _____

Closing remarks from Princess Luna

Sweet Shoppe Dreams

If you ran a Sweet Shoppe, what yummy drinks would you serve? Invent some new flavours!

_____

_____

_____

_____

_____

_____

_____

_____

_____

Decorate Your Dream Dance

At Canterlot High School, Pinkie Pie got to
decorate the gym not once, but twice!
If you were throwing your own
Fall Formal, how would you decorate it?
What would you serve?
Write some ideas here.

Refreshments:

_____

_____

_____

Decorations:

_____

_____

_____

Dance songs:

_____

_____

_____

Photograph backdrops:

_____

_____

_____

Put Your Best Hoof Forward

Design outfits for you and your friends
to attend the Fall Formal!